# THE STRAWBERRY FIELD

## SMITH MOUNTAIN LAKE

INGLATH COOPER

FENCE FREE ENTERTAINMENT, LLC

"There are moments when history turns, and we don't know it yet—but our hearts do." — **Unknown**

# PROLOGUE
## MARCH 14, 2020

**Sawyer**

The early evening traffic is locked in a stranglehold, cars honking their horns in a steady cacophony of outrage that won't change how fast we get there. An early March snow had made the streets slushy and slow-moving. I should have left the hospital earlier. But one more patient turned into five, and then there was the woman with the persistent cough, an escalating fever, and a look of panic in her eyes I couldn't ignore.

Lately, there have been more patients like her. Odd respiratory distress symptoms that hit suddenly and aren't testing positive for flu. An intensity to them that is alarming. An unusual number of pneumonia cases. As a doctor, I've never been afraid of catching illnesses from my patients. It's just not something you let yourself think about once you're committed to the field of medicine. I can't say that any longer. I'm worried. Everyone's worried.

But Michael won't be surprised I'm late. He's used to me staying too long, doing too much, never knowing when to walk away. He calls it my gift and his curse.

I check my reflection in the compact mirror. My mascara is long gone. My eyes are hollow. The freckles across my cheeks, once something I tried to cover up because they made me insecure, don't bother me tonight. It seems silly that something so inconsequential once bothered me.

That was the world I lived in a few short weeks ago. One where there wasn't something potentially terrifying looming over all of humanity, and we had time to worry about silly things like freckles. I wipe my face clean and reapply enough makeup to look as if I tried.

The black Suburban eases into a line of cars, inciting another immediate string of irritated honking.

"Sorry about the delay, ma'am," the driver says. "And the horns. New York City."

He's young. Southern drawl. Friendly, like someone raised with Sunday manners. "It wouldn't be the Big Apple without that," I say, meeting his gaze in the mirror.

"You're not from here?" he asks.

"Virginia," I tell him.

He nods. "Thought I recognized that accent. North Carolina, myself."

"What brings you north?"

"Film school. NYU. And yourself?"

"ER doc."

His brows rise. "Bet you've seen some stuff lately," he says, his voice suddenly more serious. "Any truth to what's coming out in the news?"

"I'm not sure," I say, hedging.

"Pretty scary to have people arriving in the country so sick. You think some kind of bad virus might be the real deal?"

"I think we don't know nearly enough to not take it seriously."

He nods, his forehead furrowed. "City feels different lately. Like something's coming."

I glance out the window. The sidewalks aren't as crowded as normal. Couples walk side by side, but they aren't holding hands.

It's only later I'll realize we were standing on the edge of something irreversible. A storm was coming—not sudden and dramatic, but slow, steady, and devastating, its front still hidden beyond the skyline. But the first winds were already in the air.

My phone buzzes again. Michael this time.

Got our table. Place is packed. I'll be the guy sipping a Bellini and missing you.

A stab of guilt. I reply quickly: Almost there. I'm sorry.

He always waits for me. Even when I'm hours late. Even when I don't deserve it.

We pull up to Harry Cipriani. I thank the driver and step out into the night, bracing myself against the cold air.

I walk through the narrow revolving door, a quick whirl from the angry traffic along Fifth Avenue into the luxurious interior of this exclusive Italian restaurant. It is exactly as I remembered—elegant, hushed, full of people who still look as if life isn't tilting on its axis.

Michael spots me and waves from the corner table, his smile soft and sure. As if just seeing me is all he needs.

He stands, kisses my cheek.

"Hey," I say.

"You're here."

"I am."

We sit. He asks about my day, and I answer carefully. "Busy."

I don't tell him about the young man we intubated. The grandfather who coded. The nurse who cried quietly in the break room. We both need for me to leave those things at the hospital.

"What's the occasion?" I ask.

He smiles. "I just wanted to take you somewhere nice."

But something is different in his voice. Something uncertain. Worried.

I start to ask but the waiter arrives with my Bellini. We sip, and the taste is delicious, like fresh peaches and Italy in the summertime. And then Michael raises his glass.

"Sawyer."

I meet his eyes, alarm zipping through me.

"I got offered a promotion," he says, enthusiasm in his voice. "Chicago office. It's huge. But the moment they told me, all I could think was—it doesn't mean anything if you're not there with me."

He sets down his glass, and I notice his hands are trembling, just barely.

"I want a life with you, Sawyer Blakely. All of it. The messy, unpredictable, ER doctor kind. I want the late dinners, the exhausted mornings, the missed calls. I want... you. Sawyer, I want to spend my life with you."

He reaches into his coat pocket, pulls out a small velvet box. Doesn't open it.

"There's no ring yet," he says. "I want us to choose it together. But I couldn't wait another day to ask you."

He places the box between us.

"Will you marry me, Sawyer? Will you come with me to Chicago?"

I reach for the box before I speak, my fingers brushing it, brushing his. His hand twitches beneath mine.

And something flickers in me. Not fear. Not reluctance. Just something I can't name. A seam pulling tight. A breath held too long, the weight of too many nights spent watching life and death trade places, leaving no room for promises.

"Michael. This is amazing. I'm so proud of you for getting the promotion. But leaving here. I just need some time. To think."

He nods, and his shoulders relax slightly. "Of course. I want you to be sure." He smiles again. Gentle. Hopeful.

"I'd love to build a life with you," he says. "I'd love to be the man you come home to."

I said yes, eventually. Not that night. Not with the kind of clarity or immediacy he deserved. But it doesn't matter now.

Because a few weeks after that dinner, Michael woke up with a cough. Three days later, he was on a ventilator. Four days after that, he was gone.

"Sometimes running away is the bravest thing you'll ever do."
— **Beau Taplin**

# ONE
## MAY 2020

**Sawyer**

I AM A coward.

The words lodge in my mind and begin to echo. A steady, punishing drumbeat. Coward. Coward.

The road ahead blurs. I blink hard, trying to bring it back into focus, my eyes gritty from too many nights without sleep.

Driving straight through from New York City to Smith Mountain Lake, Virginia, wasn't a great decision. But what was the alternative? Staying in the apartment that still feels like Michael will knock on the door with a pizza for my dinner after a late shift? Or drive, hour after hour, barely stopping, just enough to fill the tank, use a rest stop, scrub my hands raw, and keep going?

That's what I chose. Forward motion. Driving away on city streets quiet and unrecognizable. Restaurants boarded up, some obviously having given up for good. People standing on fire escapes just to get outside their apartments and into fresh air.

The world around me no longer feels familiar. It's as if I've been dropped into a version of life blurred just enough to make everything hard to make out. The Virginia landscape outside the car window is green, alive, but it feels as foreign as Mars. I don't trust that it won't fade before my eyes. I don't trust anything.

The events of the past three months have made that my reality.

I lower the driver's side window and stick my head out into the rushing air, letting it slap my face awake. For a moment, I feel something close to alive. Then I roll the window up and crank the air-conditioning vents toward me, welcoming the sting of cold.

I am running away.

It's not something I ever imagined doing. Not me.

Not after years of fighting for everything I built in the city, at the hospital where I once loved working. But a few months ago, I could not have imagined any of what's happened. Watching someone I loved fade with a speed I couldn't make sense of. Standing helplessly on the other side of the glass or whispering I'm sorry over and over into the beeping of machines failing to restore irreversible damage.

Medical school didn't prepare me for that. For watching death pick and choose its victims with no logic, no pattern, no mercy. For the way our ER filled with bodies faster than we could clear the hallways and the trucks at the back of the hospital serving as makeshift morgues. For the reality that there were days when we were losing more than we were saving.

At first, it looked like a bad flu. Aggressive, yes, but treatable, we thought. We started seeing patients whose lungs began to fail. By early April, we were out of ventilators and doubling patients on a single machine.

Then we started to fail, too. Breaking down under the soul-shattering weight of failure and grief.

Sweat breaks out across my forehead. My heart is racing suddenly and furiously, insisting on panic for the thoughts I am subjecting it to. I draw in a deep breath and try to push the images from my mind. Breathe in. One, two, three, four. Exhale. One, two, three, four. Repeat.

I've traveled several miles on the two-lane road before my heart slows its thumping against my chest wall. Curves have appeared, the scenery on either side of me increasingly rural. Black cows with tiny calves at their sides dot the pastures, the grass green and lush. The leaves on the hardwood trees are equally green and nearly returned from their winter retreat, startlingly alive.

The road narrows into a two-lane stretch, curving through fields and pastures. I spot cows grazing, calves nudging close to their mothers.

And I feel like a ghost drifting through it, like late fall leaves skittering on a lonely road.

It's been almost a year since I was at the lake house. After my parents died the previous summer, in a car accident that had nothing to do with the world upheaval to come, I told myself I'd visit, sort through things, decide what to do with the place. But with the onslaught of the pandemic, the grief settled on me like a second skin, too heavy to peel off. And I couldn't bring myself to come. I kept telling myself I didn't have time. Life had been turned upside down. The hospital needed me. There'd be another chance.

Then the breakdown came. That's what my therapist says happened to me. Me, shoulder everything, conquer the world me. She's right. I don't know what else to call it. Losing all ability to function as you've functioned your whole life. With drive. Purpose. Belief that your efforts matter every day. And then discovering they do not.

And now here I am. No job. No plan. Just this house, and nothing but time on my hands.

The final summer vacation we came here as a family, I was fifteen. My parents and I left that last week as three instead of four.

I try to picture Tommy's face, but the image won't come. I've attempted everything, old photos, faded memories, but it's like staring at something through a thick fog. My mind won't let me see him clearly. Maybe that's the punishment. I wasn't just the one left behind, I was part of what made him go.

My phone buzzes in the console beside me. I glance at the screen: another call from the hospital. I let it ring.

They want explanations. Clarifications. An answer to the resignation I submitted without a conversation about my decision. But I have nothing left to say. Nothing they want to hear. Nothing they don't already know.

The urge to turn around pulses sharp and sudden. Am I

running from one tragedy to the far too vivid memories of another?

But where else would I go? I don't belong in New York City anymore. And if I'm honest, I don't belong here either.

I check the GPS. I've almost reached the turnoff. The road looks different, though I'm not sure if it's the trees or the time or just me. Then I spot the mailbox. Once painted bright white. Now rusty, dented. A casualty of time and neglect.

I brake and turn the wheel, easing the car onto the pitted driveway. The first pothole is deep, filled with muddy rainwater that slaps the undercarriage and spatters the windshield. I slow to a crawl, navigating the uneven path.

The house appears at the end of the drive, just as the sky begins to dim. It looks smaller than I remember. Weather-worn. Two stories of tired brick, shutters hanging askew, paint chipped away by years of wind and rain. Sagging under its own history.

The lake is just visible through the trees, flat and colorless in the fading light.

Still. Completely still, like it, too, is holding its breath.

The air through my lowered window is warm but stale. No breeze. No sound. Not even the hum of insects.

I ease to a stop in the circular turn of the driveway. Two enormous cherry trees grace both corners of the house. They are loaded with white blooms.

I see my mother in cutoff shorts, arguing with Daddy over where to dig the holes. "Those roots are going to come for our pipes one day," he'd said.

"And you'll thank me when they bloom," she'd shot back.

Something inside me brightens at the visible evidence of life here and this piece of my mother and father that lives on. When I was young, I saw myself as a permanent fixture on this earth. But the truth I know now is we're outlived by so many things. This house has outlived my parents and my brother. And so have these trees.

Is that why I went into medicine? Because I believed I could make life last longer than it was meant to? That if I worked hard enough, cared enough, I could keep things blooming?

Maybe.

But now I know better.

Michael died in a hospital bed surrounded by machines I thought I understood. Machines I thought worthy of my trust.

I couldn't prevent his death. And neither could those machines.

None of us could.

Maybe it's fitting that it chased me back here. Because this is where I learned the truth the first time: Death doesn't care how hard you fight.

Eventually, it always wins.

## TWO

**Sawyer**

THE WHITE PAINT on the front door is chipped and peeling. The porch swing hangs crooked on rusted chains, and a few floorboards have warped upward like curled pages in an old book.

I stand there for a long moment, trying to absorb the energy of the place I once loved. Waiting for something to rise in me, nostalgia, comfort, familiarity.

But there's nothing. No warmth. No welcome.

It's as if the house has been empty for too long to remember how to offer comfort.

Or maybe it's me who's been empty for too long to receive it.

I dig out my key and unlock the door, shoulder aching under the weight of my suitcase. The air inside smells like the windows haven't been opened in years. I switch on the lights, surprised they still work, then begin opening windows one by one, trying to coax the house to breathe again.

Outside, a breeze rustles in through the screens, lifting the faded blue curtains in the living room. I inhale deeply. The scent of spring is faint but there, the sweetness of honeysuckle blooms drifting in from the vines along the driveway fence.

For the first time in months, I breathe without fear.

In New York, it felt as if I counted every inhale. Wondered what I was pulling into my lungs. Wondered if it would be the thing that finally undid me. Every breath a gamble.

Here, the air just feels like air. Clean. Familiar. And I want to cry from the relief of it, until the relief turns cruel, reminding me of everyone who'll never breathe this easily again.

But the relief is brief, and what follows is heavier, guilt, thick and immediate. It settles over me like a lead apron. My legs buckle beneath it, and I drop onto the old leather sofa by the picture window.

The cushions sigh beneath me. So do the curtains, caught again in the shifting wind.

Every part of my body feels impossibly heavy. My chest aches as if something large and immovable is sitting on it, and for a moment, I want to give in. Let the weight of survivor's guilt flatten me. Take me under.

The thought doesn't scare me. It actually comforts me.

Because maybe if I disappeared, if I slipped away into

nothingness, I could stop remembering the ones I couldn't save.

Maybe I wouldn't have to keep seeing Michael's face in his final hours, the panic in his eyes. Or hear his voice telling me he wasn't ready to go.

If I vanished, would it be like none of it happened?

Or would it just be another selfish escape?

Either way, it wouldn't matter. My failure would remain, documented in my therapist's notes, recorded in hospital reports, carved quietly into my colleagues' silence.

And worse: it would remain in me.

I can't even remember the last time I ate. Maybe yesterday? Maybe not at all during the drive. I know I had water, sipped at it like it was medicine, but I can't recall food. And yet my stomach doesn't protest. It's grown quiet lately, as if it understood there was no point in asking.

I think about the last time I stepped on a scale. Twelve pounds gone. As though the weight slipped off me when I wasn't looking. As if part of me had already started leaving before I even realized it, my clothes hanging looser, fabric brushing bone instead of skin.

I should go out. Find food. Find... something.

But the thought of it feels impossible. Right now, even standing feels impossible.

Eventually, I force myself upright. I lock the front door and leave the lights on, unwilling to let the house fall entirely into darkness. My legs are unsteady as I climb the stairs, my luggage pulling at my shoulder again.

I walk straight to the room at the end of the hall. My

childhood bedroom, where I read the Hardy Boys and Jane Austen. I open the door, half-expecting it to look different. But it's mostly the same. A little dustier. A little dimmer. But untouched in the ways that matter.

I flip on the dresser lamp and scan the room, checking corners, under the bed, behind the door. I don't know what I'm looking for. Mice? Memories?

I kick off my shoes, leave my clothes on, and collapse onto the bed. The quilt at the foot is still folded neatly. I pull it up and wrap myself inside it, cocooning until only my face remains uncovered.

The mattress yields beneath me. The ceiling fan hums.

And for one fleeting moment, I feel something that resembles safety.

Why should I be safe? Why should I be the one who made it through? I tested negative before I left New York. And yet Michael is dead.

What's fair about that?

Nothing, of course. Life isn't fair. It's random. Chaotic. Cruel.

We move through our days thinking we have some control. That if we're smart enough, careful enough, good enough, we'll be spared. But that's not how it works.

A missed step. A mistimed breath. A wrong turn. A stranger's cough.

That's all it takes.

I used to believe I was in control of my life. That if I worked hard and studied hard and stayed focused, I could bend life to my will. I actually believed I had that ability. That I had purpose.

Now I know the truth.

I control nothing. I never did.

It took an invisible enemy to teach me that.

Everything I thought I had, knowledge, skill, intuition, it failed me when it mattered most. All those years of memorizing symptoms and protocols. All the nights I spent sleepless in residency, building my endurance, proving my worth. All of it came up short.

Because when it was Michael...I couldn't save him.

And what kind of doctor can't save the person she loves?

Maybe I was never really one at all.

By degree, yes. By title, yes.

But in truth?

Doctors fight. They show up. They stay. I ran.

I'm not a doctor. Not anymore.

I'm just a woman curled under a childhood quilt, hiding from everything I couldn't fix.

"The past is never where you left it."
— **Katherine Anne Porter**

# THREE

**Sawyer**

I WAKE WITH a jolt, heart hammering. For a split second, I don't know where I am.

Sunlight spills through the window beside the bed, too bright, too sudden. I squint against it, brain scrambling until the pieces settle: Virginia. I'm at the lake house.

I collapse back onto the pillow, eyes shut tight, aching for the sleep I just left. The kind that was mercifully blank. No dreams. No memories. Just nothing. A pause from the ache.

But the light won't let me disappear again. Not today.

My stomach growls, sharp and hollow. I press a hand to the concave space beneath my ribs, startled again by the loss, of weight, of appetite, of interest in everything that used to tether me to my daily life.

Coffee. I want it so badly I can almost taste it. But I didn't bring anything with me. No groceries. No plan for any.

Even the thought of standing up feels like too much. But I move anyway.

Not from motivation, just momentum.

I strip out of yesterday's clothes and make my way to the bathroom. The faucet sputters to life, the faint sulfur smell of the well water here rising like a memory. I let it run, then step under the spray.

The heat steadies me. I scrub my skin with a bar of soap and lather shampoo through my hair. The temptation to slump against the tile overtakes me.

Back in the bedroom, I find a towel under the sink. As I press it to my face, the scent catches me—faint, but familiar. Clean linen. My mother's favorite.

For a second, I see her standing in the laundry room, pulling towels from the dryer, smiling as she scolds us for running into the lake fully clothed. Her voice echoes through my head, startlingly real.

And just like that, my throat tightens.

I blink her away and reach into my suitcase for clothes. Black yoga pants, a sports bra, a loose workout shirt. The shirt hangs on me now. Like it belongs to someone else. My reflection in the mirror is unfamiliar. Hollow cheeks. Dark smudges beneath tired eyes. Colorless lips.

The bed still looks inviting. The tousled quilt promises the kind of retreat I know too well. I take a step toward it, then stop.

Groceries. At the very least.

I grab my phone. Ten percent battery. I search for stores

nearby. Carl's Place shows up first. The name makes something small and warm flutter in my chest.

Red vinyl booths. A sticky counter. Coconut cream pie behind a glass dome, the promise at the end of a vegetable plate.

That memory pushes me down the stairs and out the door.

---

THE FUEL LIGHT blinks on as I start the car. I remember Carl's has gas, or used to. Hopefully it's still open. Not every rural place has completely reopened yet. Not every place wants to.

The road is empty, familiar in the way of things you haven't seen in years but never really forget. I reach Carl's sooner than expected.

A single truck is parked at the pump. The driver, older, baseball cap, kind eyes, nods as I pull in, tipping the brim of his hat in a quiet, politely familiar gesture.

I don't return it.

I realize that too late. And the shame that follows is instant and sharp.

I used to be better than this. Or at least I thought I was.

I grab a pair of gloves from the console and slip them on. After pumping gas, I reach for the disposable mask I brought from the city and loop it over my ears.

Inside, people come and go, unmasked, unbothered.

Their eyes land on me. Not hostile, just curious. I feel both exposed and invisible.

I want to tear the mask off, explain myself, assure them I'm not dangerous.

But fear still owns too much of me. It followed me here, and it's not letting go.

I reach for a basket and head down the far aisle.

"Morning, hon," an older woman at the dairy case says, her cart a notable mix of dried beans, eggs, and ice cream. "You new to the area, or just hiding from the world like the rest of us?"

Surprised by her friendliness, I smile behind my mask. "Little of both, I guess."

"You have a good day now," the woman says and rolls her cart on down the short aisle.

I try to remember what I came to get. Milk. Cereal. Peanut butter. Crackers. Bananas. I keep my head down, moving quickly, until I reach for a roll of paper towels and collide with someone.

I stumble back, startled.

"I'm so sorry," I say, voice muffled by the mask.

The man I've bumped into towers over me, at least six-three. I'm five-seven, and I still have to tip my head up to meet his eyes.

He steps back, giving me space.

And then I recognize him.

Jake Rowan.

My breath catches, my pulse stumbling in my throat. My

first instinct is to turn around and walk away. Pretend I didn't see him. Pretend he didn't see me.

But it's too late.

"Sawyer?"

I nod. "Jake." The name feels foreign and familiar all at once. "I... I didn't expect to see you."

"It's been a long time." His voice is quiet, even, his expression unreadable. It flows over me like warm honey, sweet with something long thought lost.

"It has."

We stand there, the silence between us thick with years and all the things we didn't say back then. Still haven't.

"Do you live here?" I ask.

"I do. You don't. At least, I didn't think you did anymore."

"I haven't been back in a while." I hesitate. "I'm—was—a physician in New York."

Alarm flickers in his eyes. "Oh—"

I rush to add, "I just got here yesterday. I tested before I left. Negative."

"I'm not worried about that. Just can't imagine what all you've seen," he says gently, shaking his head.

And I envy him, for the calm, for the steadiness, for his lack of fear.

"I never thought I'd see you again," he says.

"I never thought I'd come back."

"You haven't been back since—"

"No." My answer is sharper than I mean it to be, really. "My parents passed away last year in a car accident."

"I heard. I'm sorry about that. Really sorry." His voice

softens. The sincerity in it breaks something loose in me. A single tear escapes, disappears into the mask. I wipe at it quickly, eyes burning.

"Thank you," I say in a low voice. "I... I should pay for these."

He steps back, bumping into the cooler behind him. A Coke bottle tips and clinks gently against the others. He looks rattled.

"Okay, then," he says. "It was really nice to see you, Sawyer. I mean... sort of see you."

I almost smile. It's there, just barely. But guilt shuts it down.

"You too, Jake," I say.

At the register, the woman scans my items with practiced ease, offering a warm smile that doesn't waver at my mask or gloves. I pay quickly and murmur my thanks before heading outside.

Once I'm back in the car, I yank off the mask, toss the gloves to the passenger-side floor. My chest feels tight. My pulse skips and stutters beneath my skin.

I hate the mask. Hate the stupid gloves. I hate what they represent. Fear and everything I couldn't stop. Everything I lost.

The door to the store opens, and Jake steps out with a Coke in one hand and a small bag of cashews in the other. He's wearing neither mask nor gloves and looks as normal as if it were six months ago and life held no clues of anything so soul-destroying as a pandemic. He looks around the lot, eyes searching, uncertain, until they land on me.

Before I can start the engine, he walks toward my car. His presence feels like a reminder of another life, one where closeness wasn't dangerous.

I lower the window halfway.

"Are you okay?" he asks, voice low, gentle.

"I'm fine," I say. "Sorry."

"You don't need to apologize. You don't have to explain anything."

His words are simple, but something inside me stirs. A thread pulled taut loosens just enough. I shouldn't feel comfort in the presence of a man I haven't seen in years, not after everything. But I do.

"I just wanted you to know... if you need anything while you're here, I'm not far. I live at the old Patterson place. The one with the strawberry field behind it."

The memory hits me like a warm breeze. That field. Summer sun. Red-stained fingers. Laughter that felt like it was just a normal part of life.

"Oh," I say softly. "That's a beautiful place."

"I was lucky to get it. The owners didn't want to sell to a developer."

"I'm glad they didn't." I pause. "You've kept it the same?"

"Mostly. I fixed up the house, cleaned up the land. It feels like home now."

"How many acres?"

"Fifty. There's a strip of woods and a big pasture that used to be for cattle. I just mow it."

"That sounds... peaceful."

We fall into a pause. Not awkward. Just full. Full of questions, of curiosity, of what-ifs.

"I should go," I say finally, because really there isn't anything else to do.

"Right." He shifts his weight, hesitant. "I was going to ask... did your parents ever come back after—"

"No," I say quickly. "Not as a family. My dad came down now and then to check on things. But they never really came back. I think they meant to sell it... but they couldn't."

"I'm sorry," he says. "I shouldn't have asked."

"It's okay," I tell him. "I just... can't talk about it very easily."

"I understand," he says, stepping back. "You take care, Sawyer."

"You too."

I raise the window and start the car like something utterly terrifying is after me.

And maybe it is. Memories. Of loss. And everything I thought I left behind, but quite obviously didn't.

# FOUR

**Sawyer**

I DRIVE BACK with my hands clenched around the steering wheel, knuckles white. I force myself to let go, draw in a deep breath, and slowly pull into the driveway.

I cut the engine and sit in silence, staring at the house. The front door is still slightly ajar from earlier. The grass shimmers in the sunlight. The porch, still sagging. Everything is unchanged.

And I am exhausted.

I climb out of the car, my legs threatening to buckle. The boulder is back, lodged at the center of my chest, pressing down until it's hard to draw a full breath. I lift my bags from the back seat and carry them inside.

In the kitchen, I set them on the counter, the sound too loud in the quiet. I put the milk and half-and-half in the fridge. They sit next to a lonely yellow box of baking soda, like strangers on a train who were never meant to meet.

I slide the cereal into a cupboard, then stop, remembering I need to eat. I pull a bowl from the hutch by the screen door and pour some in, add milk, then sit at the harvest table by the window.

Outside, the lake sparkles. It's late morning now, the sun high and warm. A handful of boats crisscross the water. I spot one, low, sleek, fast. A skier cuts across the waves behind it, carving a wide arc in the still-cold water.

It's too early in the season for that. The lake has to be frigid.

But maybe the cold doesn't matter. Maybe the joy of movement, of speed, of something is worth it. I understand that. The desperate desire to feel anything but stuck.

I finish my cereal without tasting it, rinse the bowl and spoon, leave them on the counter. Then I go upstairs and pull on a pair of shorts and an old Clemson T-shirt. I don't bother with shoes.

Outside, the grass is cool beneath my feet. I follow the familiar slope of the yard down toward the dock. Two wooden chairs wait at the edge, faded, weathered, somehow still standing.

I sit in one and stretch my legs out in front of me. The sun warms my face, my shoulders. A breeze skims across the lake, brushing against my skin. I close my eyes and let myself rest there, in the quiet.

And for the first time in weeks, maybe months, I don't feel

the sharp, electric edge of fear. That knife in my nerves, always waiting, always ready. It's gone.

What's left?

I try to name the feeling. Numbness? Emptiness?

No, this is something different.

Maybe not a feeling at all. Maybe the absence of feeling.

I try to remember what used to fill me. What gave me purpose. What made me feel full.

Hope.

Yes, there was hope.

Hope for healing. Hope that when someone walks into the ER, I might be the person who could help set things right. That no matter how terrifying their detour, we could patch them up, stabilize them, and send them back out into the world to pick up where they left off.

Back then, I believed in that version of normal.

But does that word even apply anymore?

Can there be normal again?

In the rational part of my mind, I know the world will eventually find its rhythm. Humanity has weathered worse and gone on. Wars. Famine. Disease outbreaks. People will return to their lives. Children will go to school. Restaurants will reopen. The virus will shrink into something we can manage instead of something managing us.

Probably.

But I don't know if I'll be part of that world.

Will I go back? Will I return to the hospital, put the scrubs back on, walk through those doors with the same resolve I once carried?

I want to say yes.

But deep down, I know the truth. The ache of the ER lives in my bones, but the fire that once fed it is gone.

No. I won't go back.

The realization lands quietly, like a final puzzle piece sliding into place. I open my eyes and stare at the shimmering waves of the lake. The sunlight reflects hard off the surface, glinting like a spotlight on this moment of clarity.

I can't go back.

That version of me, the one who thrived in crisis, who believed in her tools, her training, her willpower, she's gone.

I don't know when exactly I lost her.

But I did.

Maybe it was the day I stood outside Michael's ICU room and realized once and for all that I was powerless. Maybe it was the night I walked out of the hospital and didn't go back. Or it could have been slower than that, a quiet crumbling over weeks on end, a soul ground down grain by grain.

Whatever the moment was, I missed it.

And now I'm left with what remains.

A shell. Brittle. Fragile.

One sharp breath away from snapping in two.

Jake's face flashes through my mind, standing beside my car, his voice soft, eyes filled with sympathy. The memory carries the faint scent of gasoline and sunlight, the sound of wind off the lake mixing with his low, steady tone. That look alone nearly shattered me.

Because with Jake came something else.

Not just kindness.

But memory. The part of my past I've worked for years to bury.

And Tommy. My brother. Whose death I couldn't process. The one no one talked about after it happened. Jake was there for all of it and seeing him brought it roaring back.

But I can't go there now. I don't have the strength to unpack that grief on top of this one.

All I know is that while I'm here at the lake, the safest thing I can do, for myself, for him, is keep my distance. Whatever once existed between us, whatever memories we share... they aren't healing. Not now.

We don't owe each other more pain.

And in a world already steeped in pain, the kindest thing I can give either of us is distance.

# FIVE

**Jake**

THIS LATE SPRING evening is the kind of night that makes enduring Virginia winters worth it.

From my back deck, I can see the faint red glow of fishing boat lights out on the lake, their motors humming softly beneath the steady chorus of frogs at the end of the cove.

The air is warm, but there's a whisper of the cool sixty-degree temperatures that will arrive by morning. Earlier, a storm rolled through—afternoon heat had climbed into the low eighties, heavy enough to break open into thunder and streaks of lightning more typical of summer than spring.

My Labrador, Hattie, had retreated to her usual storm spot under the bed. She's back out now, lying beside my chair, still wary of stray lightning. Her eyes stay half-open, ears twitching, body tight with suspicion. She hasn't quite accepted that the storm is over.

She may be right. Virginia weather doesn't play by any rules.

I reach down and scratch behind her left ear. She licks the back of my hand, then settles again, chin resting on her paws.

It's quiet now. Aside from the hum of the occasional boat engine, the night is blissfully free of distraction.

Sometimes I wonder if I should have gotten a TV. Something to break the silence.

But then I think of the news, and my stomach turns.

Once you've heard your name on a broadcast, attached to a story built on rumor and outrage, you stop thinking of the news as company.

I pick up my beer on the side table, take a long pull. Still cold enough. I close my eyes, but I can still hear her voice. The reporter. I remember every word. The accusations. The fallout. The way my life unraveled in slow motion while the world watched.

I shake the memory off, reach over, and turn on the radio. A classic country station hums to life, delivering an upbeat song meant to take you back to high school Saturdays, windows down, music up, nothing in the world but freedom.

I lean back, let it wash over me. I try to find a memory like that, something light and unburdened.

But they're slippery now.

Distant.

Like they belong in someone else's life.

I stare out at the lake. The dark water. The flicker of reflected light.

And I wonder, has the man they painted me to be erased my history?

Did their words steal my own memories of who I was?

I wasn't raised with much. I worked for everything. Grants. Loans. Long hours. I put myself through college, through grad school. A doctorate in economics. All of it built from scratch.

And what good did any of it do?

Sometimes I wonder if I would've been better off following my mom's path. A job where your paycheck doesn't depend on reputation. Where no one can accuse you of something you can't prove you didn't do. Where your life doesn't implode from the opinions of strangers.

But the past doesn't let you rewrite it.

You live. You learn. You course-correct where you can.

That's what I tried to do, build something new. Something quieter. A life that doesn't hinge on anyone else's approval.

I was once social. Friends. Parties. A string of relationships that never quite fit. I kept waiting for the one that would. For the person who would match me. Mirror me. See past my flaws and name them as strengths.

Someone like Sawyer.

Because if I'm honest, she did. Long ago.

Maybe I would have found someone else like her, eventually. But I stopped looking.

You stop wanting to be known when you're afraid of what people will see.

And maybe that's the part of me that died, the part that

wanted to be chosen for who I was before everything changed.

I reach down and run my hand across Hattie's soft head. I'm not lonely, not really. Not in the way people think of it. I've made peace with solitude. I think the part of me that craved companionship, marriage, family, a life with someone by my side, burned out when I saw myself reflected in the headlines.

When I looked into the eyes of students who used to admire me—and found wariness instead.

No one looks at me that way now. And when I look in the mirror, I see what they saw.

I've been through every stage of grief. Anger. Denial. And now... acceptance.

This is my life. Not the one I chose, but one I've carved out of the ruins. And in many ways, it's a good life. A quiet one. A stable one.

I'm grateful for my economics education and the interest I'd always had in investing. That backup plan, the one I never thought I'd need, is what let me walk away when I had to. It's what let me buy this farm. The house. The strawberry field out back. The acres of land that don't ask questions and don't pass judgment.

It was a significant purchase. But I needed to put my money somewhere solid. Into something no one could take from me unless God Himself came down and took it.

Because I'm done putting my life in the hands of other people's opinions.

Now I spend my days tending the soil. Watching something grow from nothing. The strawberries are stubborn but beautiful. They'll ripen mid-May to early June, bright red, messy. For a few brief weeks, they'll become something that feels like art.

And then they'll be gone. But certain to appear again next year. Reliable as only nature can be.

Maybe that's all we can hope for in this life. That something we create, something we love, leaves a mark. Even if it doesn't last forever.

I think of Sawyer again. How many times I've imagined seeing her. How often I've played out the possibility.

Always knowing it would never happen.

And then yesterday, there she was. At a country store. On the heels of something I never imagined living through.

Why now?

Why her?

Hope flickers. Something I thought I'd put away long ago. I let it breathe for half a second, then douse it with the cold water of reality. That will never happen.

Thunder rumbles somewhere in the distance. Lightning flashes briefly over the lake.

Hattie shivers and whines, as unsettled by the storm's appearance as I am by running into the girl, now a woman, I once imagined spending my life with.

I stand, pat my leg, wanting to reassure her even if I can't reassure myself. "Come on, Hattie. Let's go inside. You're safe. I've got you."

*Twenty-five Years Ago*

TOMMY AND I met the summer we both worked at Smith Mountain Dock. Our jobs there started when school let out. First weekend of June for me, second weekend of that month for Tommy. His family came to the lake from Charlottesville for the summer, and we were assigned to the gas pumps, filling tanks, tying up boats, and flirting with whoever drifted in.

Well, Tommy flirted. I mostly watched.

He had the kind of smile that made girls forget whatever they were saying mid-sentence. Naturally confident, charming. I didn't mind fading into the background. I was shy, and it gave me space to learn his rhythm.

One afternoon, a girl invited us to a party. Her name was Bethany, blonde, cute, loud, a girl who wasn't used to being told no. Her parents were out of town. The party was at their lake house. It was the kind of situation you know is a bad idea and go anyway because everyone else is.

Tommy drove that night, picking me up at my house just after seven o'clock. I had my license as well, but no car to drive yet, so I was happy to bum the ride from him in the Jeep his parents gave him for his sixteenth birthday. On the drive to Bethany's place, he left the top down and cranked the music. The big Bose speakers Tommy installed in the back of the Jeep blasted AC/DC, and I remember thinking how great it was to be nearing adulthood with all its infinite possibilities and to have found a new friend as great as Tommy.

I'd had plenty of friends at Franklin County High School.

I played on the football team, not in any capacity that would set state records, but respectably. There had been something about my last year in school, though. Maybe it was the fact that I had as much desire to lose myself in a book at lunchtime as to talk about plays for the following weekend's upcoming football game.

Whatever the reason, there hadn't been anyone I could call a best friend. Tommy was someone I had more than just the surface stuff in common with. He liked books and learning, too. And while I had every reason to suspect his family life was a lot easier than mine, both relationship-wise and materialistically, none of that seemed to matter when it came to the ease with which we were able to talk to each other about stuff I didn't talk to anyone else about.

After hanging out a couple of times, it became clear to me that Tommy didn't need to get raging drunk to have a good time. Some of my friends from high school did, although I still hadn't figured out how a massive hangover the next morning was necessary to have fun on the weekend.

The clincher for me on the subject of alcohol had been my brother's DUI and subsequent jail time just after his eighteenth birthday.

He'd had a head-on one Saturday night on 122 after leaving a party around two a.m., smashing into a woman taking her elderly grandmother to the hospital in the middle of the night for an asthma attack. He'd nearly killed both of them, and as far as I could see, it was by the grace of God that he had escaped vehicular homicide. That experience had jackhammered fear into the core of me.

It just wasn't worth the risk.

And so, that night at the party when Tommy decided to have a few beers, I volunteered to be the designated driver. We stayed at Bethany's until almost twelve-thirty. My curfew was one o'clock, so I went looking for Tommy, finding him upstairs in Bethany's bedroom with the door cracked. When I stuck my head in, it was to see Tommy and Bethany making out on her bed. Tommy raised up on one elbow. "That you, Jake?"

"Yeah," I called out from behind the now-closed door, dropping my head back and staring at the ceiling. "Sorry, man," I said, "but I've got to get home."

"Ask your mom if you can crash at my place."

So I asked, and to my surprise, she said yes, half asleep, probably, and not in the mood to argue. I waited downstairs until Tommy reappeared, hair a little tousled, grin sheepish.

He tossed me the keys. "You drive. I've had a little too much."

I slid under the wheel, excited to be driving something other than my mom's Chevrolet station wagon. Tommy gave me directions to his house as I drove. With the top down, the night air was cooler than earlier, but it still felt great, and I remember thinking as we rolled down the two-lane country road that it was damn great to be young and alive and able to go out on a Saturday night with a friend.

I'd never been to Tommy's house by road. I'd seen it from the water, but it was a beautiful old place, the house handed down from his grandfather. He had told me one afternoon that his parents had renovated it, and that he secretly liked all the new creature comforts over the version his mother had lovingly referred to as stepping back in time. Whatever it was called, I'd known when we stepped inside the foyer that night it was, indeed, a home. There was the lingering smell of baking in the air, something like chocolate chip cookies or banana bread. My stomach had rumbled, and I remembered not eating dinner that night. My mom had been home from work when I left, and the refrigerator empty except for a couple slices of hardened American cheese and a bottle of mustard.

Tommy made straight for the kitchen, waving for me to follow, even as he gave me the "Shh" sign so we wouldn't wake up his family. The lights were off, and he flipped on the switch as we walked into the room.

A pretty girl sat on the barstool at the counter, her plate filled with what looked like a half-eaten slice of apple pie, a dollop of vanilla ice cream melting down the sides.

"Hey, sis," Tommy said, making a beeline for the refrigerator. "What are you doing up?"

"Waiting for you," she said, taking another bite of her pie.

"Told you I'd be late," he said.

"I know," she said.

"Jake, this is Sawyer, my sassy baby sister. Sawyer, Jake."

"Hey," I said.

"Hey," she said back. "And I'm not a baby."

Tommy had already told me that his sister was fifteen, but if I hadn't known that, I would have guessed she was older. She was mature for her age, both in posture and looks, and I found myself glancing away and not meeting eyes with her, the same way I did when the popular girls in high school tried to talk to me at lunch.

"Where'd y'all go?" she asked.

"To a party," Tommy said, pulling stuff from the well-stocked refrigerator and placing it on the island countertop across from Sawyer.

"You want a sandwich, Jake?" Tommy asked.

"Yeah," I said, hoping I didn't sound too eager.

He opened a drawer, pulled out two knives, and handed me one. "Make yourself at home," he said. "I'm having turkey and cheese. There's some other stuff here, so just make what you like."

"Thanks," I said, appreciating again Tommy's easygoing generosity. I felt awkward and clumsy with Sawyer watching. But I was too hungry to concede to vanity, so I continued on following Tommy's lead until I'd built myself a towering sandwich that had to be cut into quarters so I could eat it. Tommy dug into his, and I followed suit. Neither of us said anything until we had finished half.

"Whose party?" Sawyer asked.

"Bethany's."

"Bethany's," she repeated.

"What?" Tommy said. "You don't even know her."

"I don't have to," Sawyer said, taking another bite of her pie. "How many Bethanys have you known?"

"A few," Tommy conceded with a smile.

"That's an understatement," she said. And then looking at me directly, "Do you like girls like Bethany, Jake?"

Any response I could think of stuck in my throat. I was

older and supposedly more mature and should be able to navigate my way through a conversation with Tommy's younger sister. But there was something about her that made me tongue-tied to say the least, and I shrugged.

"No?" she asked.

"I don't know," I answered, wiping my mouth with a paper napkin Tommy pulled from a drawer. "I guess I wonder what do you mean by girls like Bethany?"

"Girls who don't exactly play hard to get," she said without hesitating.

Tommy laughed. "Sawyer, what do you know about it? Have you been reading Mom's 1950s romance novels again?"

"Shut up, Tommy," she said, half smiling.

"Well, believe me," Tommy said. "It doesn't happen in real life like it happens in those books."

Sawyer rolled her eyes. "So how does it happen?"

I sat there and watched the exchange between the two, admittedly envious. They teased each other, but the love between them was clear, even to me when I'd barely been around them long enough to know. I knew how it was between me and my brother and the fact that I had been a nuisance to him. What would it be like to have a sibling who had your back, who cared if you messed up or made mistakes? Who tried to set a good example for you.

"There are plenty of girls who like you, Tommy, that aren't like Bethany."

"Oh, yeah? Well, sis, right now, I'm perfectly fine with the Bethanys of the world."

"You better not get her pregnant. Daddy will kill you."

"Sawyer!" Tommy said, looking up and shooting her a look of disapproval. "Where the heck did that come from?"

"I saw the condoms in your nightstand drawer," she said, back to eating her pie with deliberation.

"What were you doing in my nightstand drawer?"

"I was looking for a pen, but found something other than that, obviously."

"Well then," he said, "at least you know I have no intention of getting anyone pregnant."

"If you're old enough to be having sex," she said, "then I guess you're old enough to know they're not foolproof."

"Yes, Mom," he said. "I am aware they're not foolproof."

Tommy looked at me then. "Do you have brothers and sisters, Jake, that give you grief like this?"

I shook my head. "I have a brother. But he doesn't care what I do."

"Lucky you," Tommy said. But that was where I had to disagree with him. I didn't think it made me lucky at all.

---

AFTER THAT NIGHT, Sawyer started showing up at the dock when Tommy and I were working, riding a family Sea-Doo over. At first, she had some reason for being there. She'd come by to get some food from the snack bar, fill up the Sea-Doo with gas, and then when she seemed to run out of new excuses, she started hanging out and watching while we filled boats with gas, sipping on a Dr. Pepper from the snack bar fountain.

Tommy was usually busy talking to whichever girl happened to be hitting on him at the moment, and so Sawyer began talking to me. At some point, it started to become obvious that she was coming to see me and not Tommy. I'd been flattered by this even though Sawyer was two years younger. She was pretty. Really pretty. And I had the impression that this was something she hadn't been aware of until recently. I didn't know whether she had reached this conclusion on her own or if she'd picked up on my reluctant attraction. And it was that. Reluctant. Very.

I clearly understood the age difference between us, as well as the value of my friendship with Tommy, and there was no way I was going to do anything to cross either one of those lines, but Sawyer was just easy to talk to. She seemed to be interested in my answers to the questions she asked of me: What did I want to do when I got out of high school? What was the best book I'd ever read? Did I think it was a bad thing for football players to get concussions on a regular basis? Did I think people needed to eat meat in order to be healthy?

That was the question she'd asked me one hot July afternoon when Tommy was again flirting with a girl from North Carolina there for the week with her family. Sawyer was sitting on the edge of the dock, just down from the gas pump I was in charge of manning. She dangled her feet in the water, tossing bits of bread from her peanut butter and jelly sandwich to the ducks hovering a few feet away.

"Because," she said, "you see, I don't think so. I keep looking for books in the library that talk about how much protein people need and what kind, and I haven't read anything yet that convinces me we have to get it from eating animals. What do you think?"

"I guess I never thought about it," I said, feeling her passion.

"I don't think most people ever have," she said without any criticism in her voice. Her tone was considering, as if she were wading through the logic right then and there with me. "For example, we've given names to foods that don't say what it is we're eating, like a hamburger is not called 'cow shoulder'. Do you think people would eat it if it was called that?"

"Uh, no," I said.

"And bacon. I mean, what does bacon have to do with what you're eating?"

"I guess that's the whole idea," I said. "So people can deceive themselves."

Things were slow, so I closed the gap between us and sat down next to her on the dock.

"Don't you think a lot of things in life are like that?" she said. "We don't want to look at the truth, so we call it something else or put a label on it that hides what it is."

"Maybe," I said. "What's got you thinking about all this?"

She lifted her shoulders and shrugged. "When I was a girl, and we would drive down here to visit, we used to pass all these pastures full of cows grazing. They'd have babies by their sides, and the babies would be running around playing in the grass. I used to think it was such an amazing sight, that maybe that's what heaven would be like. It was something I looked forward to about the drive down here. But then one weekend we drove by this farm, and there was a tractor-trailer backed up in the middle of the field. They had this section of gates that made a big square around it. They were chasing the cows into the enclosure and onto the back of the truck. Some of the older babies weren't being allowed to get on the truck, just the mamas and I asked Daddy where they were taking them and why they wouldn't let all of them get on. I remember it took him a moment to answer me, but he's always tried to tell me the truth even when he didn't want to. When he told me where they were taking them, I started screaming and rolled down the window and stuck my head out and yelled at the people to stop. Daddy drove on faster because I guess he didn't want the people to think I'd lost it, but then I started begging him to go back and buy all the cows so they wouldn't have to go there. He told me that he couldn't do that and it wouldn't matter anyway because if people want to buy hamburgers and steaks, that's what's going to happen to cows. I didn't speak to him for a week, I was so angry at him. It took me that long to admit he was right. It made me angry at the whole world. I still am. Angry."

    I stared at her, noting the way she wouldn't look up at me, her shoulders stiff and rigid as she stared down at her feet in the water. I could tell she was waiting for my answer and that what I said would make or break her. I didn't want to answer her because I didn't want that kind of power. I just knew that she cared what I thought. And so I considered my answer before saying, "I think, Sawyer, that's one of the most awful things about growing up and not being a kid anymore. The realization that there are some things in this world that we don't see the way other people see them. That some of those things we're never going to change. That maybe all we can do is live our version of truth and what we believe is right to the best of our ability. And even that won't be perfect. But what if everyone did their part in making the world a compassionate place? Wouldn't that add up to things being drastically different?"

She did look at me then, our eyes meeting and holding before she said, "Yeah. I think it would."

And it was in that moment on that hot, summer afternoon that I think we both realized we saw in each other some reflection of ourselves that maybe no one else had ever seen. Or maybe we'd never let anyone else see for fear of being judged or ridiculed. And even though there was still a shimmer of tears in her eyes, Sawyer had smiled at me. The thing I could compare it to was the sun rising in the sky after days and days of rain. I felt the connection between us click into place, life-changing and permanent.

When I think of that day now, it's the stillness that haunts me, the way the fog on the lake never lifted, just hovered there, blurring the edges of everything. Maybe that's how grief works. It hides what's too painful to look at until you're ready to see it again. I wonder if that's what Sawyer's been trying to do all these years, see her brother's face through the fog and not the loss.

# SIX

**Sawyer**

I WAKE TO the sun again, squinting at my phone screen on the nightstand next to the bed. This time it's morning. Nine o'clock. I'd gone to bed around six, sleeping another fifteen hours without waking a single time, my body fatigued to the bone. I drop back onto the pillow, listening for my own feelings of energy this morning. The dead weight of the fatigue I've felt for weeks now seems to have lifted a bit, the breath in my chest a little lighter. Not enough to feel like myself, just enough to notice the difference.

I try to think of what I should do today, focus my thoughts on the possibility of walking through the house and making a to-do list of everything that needs to be done to prepare it for sale. Just the thought, though, settles another boulder of anxiety on my chest. I focus instead on the prospect of coffee, sitting up. I slip on the pair of bedroom slippers I had brought with me and pad down the stairs to the kitchen.

Within a few minutes, the room smells of coffee, and I pour a cup, taking a tentative sip without adding the cream and sugar I normally prefer. Surprisingly, the taste is delicious, and I decide to forge ahead with the black coffee. Something about denying myself the simple comfort of cream and sugar feels fitting, though it does nothing to change the fact that I've walked away from my life's work. Still, standing here with a warm cup in my hands feels… tolerable. More tolerable than anything has in a long while.

I open the refrigerator and pull out the loaf of whole wheat bread I bought at Carl's yesterday, dropping two pieces into the toaster on the kitchen counter. I go back for the butter, and then wait for the toast to brown, sipping at my coffee. Jake pops into my mind. And I realize the reason I had gone to bed so early the night before was to stop myself from thinking about him. Yet, here I am again, his face as clear in my mind as if he were standing right before me. It had taken me years to stop thinking about him. The thought doesn't hurt the way everything else does. Not today.

Not so surprising, given that I had, early on in our friendship, decided that he was the one for me, despite the two years separating us that first summer we met. I found in Jake a simpatico I had never known with anyone else in my life, other than my brother. And that was different. That was different.

*Twenty-five Years Ago*

IT WASN'T THAT Jake ever gave me a reason to believe he liked me that way. He didn't. In fact, he was frustratingly careful, always holding me at arm's length. No matter how many summer afternoons I spent trying to get closer, he never crossed that invisible line between us. Tommy teased me relentlessly about my crush on Jake. "Little sis," he said one afternoon as we sat on the dock. "You know he can't like you like that, right? Y'all are in different phases." We'd been sitting on the dock on a summer afternoon when he hadn't been working. A thunderstorm hung in the distant sky, and I had known just from the regular patterns of our summer days that the rain would be arriving soon. Rolling my eyes, I said, "What about you and that eighteen-year-old you were hanging out with a couple of years ago?" "She was legal," he said with a smirk. "Old enough to make her own choices."

"It's only two years, Tommy," I shot back. "Why does that make it such a big deal?"

"It's just that he's older than you. I don't think our parents would be thrilled about that."

"You don't know what they'd think."

"I do," he said. "You're their little girl."

"I don't want to be their little girl," I snapped, crossing my arms. The words came out angry, but what followed was worse, a lump in my throat, hot tears sliding down my cheeks. I hated that he saw them. That he saw me.

"Aw, hey now," Tommy said gently. "I didn't mean to make you cry."

"You didn't," I mumbled, turning away.

"You're hung up on him."

I didn't answer. I didn't have to.

"Has he said anything to make you think—"

"No." I wiped at my face. "He hasn't. He's done nothing wrong."

"I didn't think so. Jake's a good guy."

"I know."

Tommy put a hand on my shoulder, gave it a quick squeeze. "I get it. I do. But you know it can't happen. Not right now."

I wanted to scream at the unfairness of it. At time itself, at age, at everything that stood between us.

"I didn't ask to feel this way about him," I whispered.

"I know," Tommy said. "Love doesn't work like that. The lightning bolt strikes wherever it wants."

We sat in silence, the storm inching closer. The sky had darkened, the air charged and restless.

"Might be a good idea to take some space," he said eventually. "Maybe... don't see him for a while."

The suggestion knocked the wind out of me.

Jake was the closest I'd come to feeling like someone saw the parts of me I didn't have to explain. The sensitive parts. The soft-hearted parts. I didn't have to shield those with him.

But I knew Tommy was right.

"Maybe," I said quietly.

"Call some friends from school. See if anyone wants to come down for a visit."

"Yeah. Maybe."

"I can give Jake a heads-up, if that'd make it easier."

"No," I said quickly, emotion tightening my throat so that I can barely get out a whispered, "He won't even notice I'm not around."

"That's not true," Tommy said. "You're a stunner, sis. And you two have this weird intelligentsia vibe going on."

"He's smart," I murmured. "And kind."

"So are you."

Thunder rumbled across the lake. The clouds hovering above us now were darker, ominous-looking. Smith Mountain stood majestic and deep green across the wide expanse of lake. A splat of rain dropped onto the dock, then another, and another and then began to pour. Tommy got up from his chair and held out his hand.

"Come on, we need to get inside."

"No," I said. "You go. I'll be up in a minute."

"Sawyer—"

"I will. I promise."

He nodded, gave me one last look, and jogged toward the house.

But I didn't follow.

I stayed on the dock as the storm rolled in. Rain pounded my head, streamed down my face, soaked through my clothes.

And I let it.

Some part of me wanted the lightning to find me. To end the ache before it grew into something I'd have to carry for years.

But fate didn't have that in mind for me either. So when the clouds parted, and the sun slid back across the sky, I was still sitting there, raw with the new awareness of just how long the summer would be, now that it was going to be measured in days of not seeing Jake.

# SEVEN

**Sawyer**

BY MY THIRD cup of coffee, the silence is too loud. I start the list.

I open the Notes app on my phone and give it the uninspired title: To-Do. Then, still in my pajamas, I begin walking through the house.

Most of the windows are cloudy with grime, years of weather clinging to the glass.

Call window washer.

The living room, kitchen, main hallway, and foyer all need paint.

Call painter.

At least a dozen light bulbs are out.

Buy light bulbs. Me.

The carpets are dusty, edges curled from neglect.

Vacuum. Me.

I head outside for the exterior walk-through, still in slippers, my coffee cooling in my hand. The outside is worse. The windows need repainting.

Call painter—again.

From the yard, I spot a few shingles missing on the roof.

Call roofer. Check for leaks.

The trees have grown wild, branches dipping dangerously close to the power lines.

Call tree service.

The grass is patchy and brown in places. The landscaping company my father used is clearly still in place but no longer trying.

Call landscaper. Request fertilizer and reseed.

I make my way toward the back of the property, following the flagstone path to the dock. The lake is calm this morning, the light low and golden. The dock, however, is in rough shape. Paint is peeling, and several floorboards are warped beyond salvage.

Call carpenter. Replace dock boards.

Green algae climbs the posts near the waterline.

Call pressure washer.

Two old wooden chairs still sit at the edge of the dock, their once-smooth arms bleached and split from sun and rain. They look... tired.

I picture my parents sitting here. I hear the soft murmur of their voices, see their silhouettes in fading light, wine glasses resting on the wide chair arms. I remember the way my mother leaned into my father's shoulder. The way he always glanced at her when she laughed.

They talked often about retiring here. After Tommy and I left home. They planned for it. Dreamed of it.

The memory hits me so hard now it nearly knocks the breath from my lungs.

Tears rise fast. I wipe them away with the back of my hand, but more follow.

I haven't let myself think about them recently. I've kept the grief boxed up, hidden behind the urgent chaos of hospital shifts and then the fog of Michael's death. But it's here now. Just beneath the surface.

A shallow grave.

And it doesn't take much to dig through.

Loneliness wraps around me, heavy and absolute. At my age, it wouldn't be unusual to have a family, a partner, children, a small circle of people to love and protect.

But I chose differently.

Or maybe life chose for me.

I gave everything to my career, and now the career is gone. The people I loved are gone. I wonder what it would feel like to be worried right now, not just for myself, but for someone else. For children. For a husband.

Maybe I'm lucky.

Maybe it's easier not to love anyone when everything is falling apart.

I lower myself into one of the dock chairs. The morning sun is warm on my face. I close my eyes.

I think of the patients I've watched die these past months, so many of them elderly, scared, alone. I think of the families who loved those people, and how horrible it had been for them not to be with their loved one when they passed away, both for the family members and the patients. The desperate phone calls, the impossible decisions, the unbearable goodbyes spoken over speakerphones.

It is truly unthinkable that we are living in a world that looks so unfamiliar, a world where you might have to die alone, except for heavily masked and protected nurses and doctors who know you as sick and helpless.

And the people trying to save you, they're barely hanging on, too.

Logically, I know my breakdown isn't surprising. I saw it happening around me, even in the strongest colleagues. At first, we coped. ER doctors are no strangers to death. We process. We move on.

But this wasn't death as we knew it. This was wave after wave of helplessness.

Patients kept coming. And coming. And we kept failing.

Eventually, you stop believing the next one can be saved. And that's when something inside you dies too.

I used to believe I went into emergency medicine to make a difference. To be the one standing in the storm, keeping the worst from happening. But deep down, it was always about Tommy. Trying to save people the way no one could save him.

And maybe, for a while, I did make a difference. Maybe enough to count for something.

But not anymore.

I won't go back.

Not to medicine. Not to that version of myself.

I know this now with a clarity that startles me.

I'm spent.

Hollowed out.

And if I'm honest, I'm not sure what comes next.

Maybe this, fixing up the house, a checklist of repairs, isn't about selling the place.

Maybe it's just the one thing I can still do for my parents, the last thing.

I can restore what they loved.

Make it beautiful again.

Make it ready for someone else to love.

So I stand. Walk back to the house. And I begin to make the calls.

# EIGHT

**Jake**

THE STRAWBERRY FIELD stretches in front of me, five acres of low green plants and pink-tinted berries beginning to swell under spring sunlight.

In one hand, I hold a five-gallon sprayer. In the other, a hoe. Hattie sits beside me, her ears up, tail wagging, eyes full of her usual question: What are we doing next?

"Come on, girl," I say. "Let's get to it."

Today I'm spraying the berry vines. The mix is organic and non-toxic, citronella-based, pleasant-smelling, and designed to deter the insects eager to burrow into the fruit just as it ripens. It's been my goal from the start: create a safe, chemical-free farming environment.

It's never made sense to me to spray food with chemicals that not only kill bugs who might be trying to find a meal on the plants but also do undeniable harm to the people who end up eating the berries. I walk between the vines, spraying left, then right. The process will take most of the morning, but I consider it well worth the effort.

Hattie trots ahead, occasionally shaking her head at the fly that keeps landing between her ears. I move slowly down the rows. When I spot a weed, I stop and take the hoe to its roots.

It's quiet work. Steadying. The berries should fully ripen in another few weeks. If we're lucky and the weather holds.

It's been a mild spring. It's been a gift to have something to do outdoors. To keep moving. To breathe.

I reach the end of the row, and there's nothing left to keep my thoughts from going where they've been trying to go all morning.

Sawyer.

I tried to keep her out of my head, but now I let her in.

Seeing her yesterday had rattled me more than I wanted to admit. I'd gone to Carl's to grab a few things, and she was the last person I expected to see.

She'd looked up and recognized me, and for a moment, I saw her emotions flash wide across her face before she locked them down.

I'll admit—curiosity got the better of me long before yesterday. I'd looked her up once or twice. Social media. A few photos: beach trips, running races, a clean white coat and confident smile. She looked strong. Alive. The Sawyer I remembered, only more herself.

But the woman I saw yesterday...

That wasn't the Sawyer I remembered.

She looked thinner than she should be. Pale. Her hair hung limp around her shoulders, like it hadn't been washed in a few days. But it was her eyes that stayed with me.

Haunted.

Like she'd seen something too awful to speak of—and hadn't yet found a way to live with it.

I know her parents died last year. Maybe that's it.

But I wonder if there's more.

I thought about sending a card. But the bridge between Sawyer and me is long and cracked, and I didn't know how to cross it.

That summer, we were young. Naive in every way that matters. We thought the future was ours to shape. I never imagined the life I have now. I doubt she imagined hers would lead to whatever weight I saw in her yesterday.

The age difference scared me back then. Two years is nothing now, but when you're seventeen and she's just turned fifteen, it might as well be a canyon. Still, the connection was there. Real. Immediate.

Too real.

Tommy had no idea what he introduced when he brought me into his world. He never imagined a spark would form between his best friend and his little sister.

And I never acted on it.

But I thought about it.

And maybe that's enough to taint it in hindsight.

I hoe a weed too aggressively, slicing through the soil. Hattie glances at me, ears twitching. She picks up on the shift in my mood. She always does.

"It's all right," I murmur, softening my voice. She relaxes, wagging her tail once before continuing on ahead.

I wish people were as forgiving as dogs. As simple. The world would be a better place for it.

It's been a long time since I wanted anything more than what I have here. This life, quiet, self-contained, private, suits me. There's no one looking at me with questions in their eyes. No one wondering if the rumors were true.

I know what people see when they look me up online.

And no matter what I say, doubt will always linger.

Because that's the world now.

The louder story wins.

The news tells its social media-polished version with a smile, then moves on to the next wreckage. They don't look back to see what's been left behind.

I could be bitter.

And some days, I am.

But I refused to let bitterness consume me. That was the one piece of ground I could still claim. I built this life out of what remained. And for the most part, it's enough.

I finish the last row, drop the sprayer, and wipe sweat from my brow with my sleeve. The sun is strong today, the first full-sun day in a week.

Sawyer drifts back into my mind.

I wonder how long she'll be here. Whether I'll see her again.

I assume not. That's probably best.

A horn sounds at the top of the driveway. Hattie barks, tail up, ears forward.

The UPS truck rumbles in, dust blooming behind it. The driver, brown mask, quick wave, jumps down with a package and places it beneath the big oak tree. He returns with three more, shouts a cheerful have a good day, and rolls back down the drive.

And just like that, my human interaction for the day is over.

A pang hits, sharp and unexpected.

Loneliness. I haven't felt it in so long that I almost don't recognize it. The weight of it settles in my chest like humidity before a storm.

But I know where it came from.

Seeing Sawyer.

She's from a time when I believed life might look different than it does now. A time when I still hoped for something more than solitude and land and the quiet company of a dog.

Regret nips at the edges of my thoughts.

Not for my choices.

But for what never had the chance to become anything at all.

I don't know what Sawyer's carrying, but I saw the weight in her.

And it didn't look any lighter than mine.

There was something about her yesterday, something unspoken but undeniable.

Recognition of history. A quiet grief.

And I still see it in her. I feel the pull. The temptation to reach out.

But I don't move.

Because I know better. I've lived long enough to understand that some things are best left alone.

I would rather she remember me as the boy who wanted her, but said no.

And not the man the world has told her I became.

# NINE

**Sawyer**

I'M IN THE bathtub when I see it.

A blur of movement, quick and dark, just at the edge of my vision. I bolt upright, heart hammering, water sloshing. Grabbing a towel, I scramble out of the tub, dripping, breath shallow, skin cold. I stand on the toilet lid, scanning the corners of the bathroom, willing it to be my imagination.

But it's not.

There's movement near the base of the wooden shelf where I keep the towels. I take a cautious step down, praying I'm far enough away that it won't bolt.

I grab my phone, turn on the flashlight, and shine it at the bottom of the shelf.

There it is. Coiled. Still. And, for now, silent.

My worst fear. A snake.

I leap across the room, fling the door shut behind me, and

jam the towel underneath the crack at the bottom to keep it from escaping. My hands are shaking. My skin prickles with panic.

How did it get in?

Could there be more?

A family?

I try to breathe. Try not to hyperventilate.

But I know one thing with certainty: I can't handle this alone.

Still wrapped in a towel, I change clothes quickly and sit on the edge of the bed, phone in hand, searching.

Snake removal. Local wildlife control. Anything.

I find a service in Roanoke. Leave a message. Then another in Lynchburg. Same result. No answer. No help.

Frustrated, I toss my phone beside me on the bed and lie back, trying to hold still, trying not to think of what's behind that door.

But of course, I do.

And that's when Jake's name floats up.

I hesitate.

A hundred reasons why not to call him race through my mind.

But desperation has a way of dulling pride.

I search his name in the local listings—nothing. I remember the name of the farm he bought, and I know the road. I know the house. I know the strawberry field.

I've known it my whole life.

I throw on sandals, grab my phone and keys, and head out the door.

The drive is short. Familiar. The road lined with memories. New houses dot the area now, but the old landmarks are still there. Still standing.

The turnoff to Jake's comes sooner than I expect. I brake hard, tires squealing a little on the gravel. I wince, hoping no one saw that.

The strawberry field comes into view first, lush, green, vibrant with impending fruit. A pang hits me. I remember walking these rows with my mother, her hands full of strawberries meant for pies and jam.

The house appears next. It's beautiful. Cared for. Alive.

Unlike mine.

A yellow Lab barks and trots toward the Jeep, tail wagging. I sit still for a moment, then step out. The gravel crunches beneath my feet.

Jake appears in the doorway, clearly surprised. His expression shifts quickly to something neutral. I fumble for words.

"I'm sorry for dropping by like this," I say, feeling incredibly awkward.

"Hattie," he says, and the dog stops barking at once. Her tail still wags, and she ambles over, sniffing my knee. I rub beneath her chin, and she presses against me, all trust and softness.

It's disarming.

So is he.

"Is everything okay?" Jake asks, closing the distance between us.

"I'm sorry," I repeat. "I tried finding a number for you,

but... I didn't know who else to call. I tried some wildlife services, but no one answered."

He steps closer, brows furrowed. "What happened?"

I hesitate, then blurt it out. "There's a snake. In my bathroom."

Jake's face shifts. For a moment, I think he might laugh. Then a smile breaks across his face, and despite myself, I smile too.

"You want help getting it out?"

"Would you? Please? I've managed to handle a lot of things in life, but snakes are not one of them."

"No problem," he says easily. "I'll follow you over."

"You don't mind? I feel awful asking you."

"I don't mind at all. Come on, Hattie." He whistles, and she trots after him to a dusty Ford truck with Farm Use plates. "We'll see you there."

---

I DRIVE BACK to the house, Jake's truck following close behind. In my rearview mirror, I watch Hattie with her head out the window, ears flapping. Like a second passenger.

There's something about Jake's ease that undoes me a little. I'd forgotten this about him, his ability to lessen awkwardness, to dissolve embarrassment with kindness. There are people who pounce on vulnerability, who use it as leverage. Jake never did. He never made me feel small.

We arrive within minutes. I park. He pulls in beside me. Hattie jumps out, tail wagging.

Jake opens the tailgate and pulls out a long silver tool.

"What's that?" I ask.

"Snake tongs. One of humanity's finest inventions."

"Where'd you get those?"

"Hardware store. Had a mama rat snake in my potting shed once. Didn't want to kill her, but I sure didn't want her staying. And no, it won't hurt the snake."

"Good to know."

"Mind if Hattie comes in?"

"Of course not."

We enter the house, head upstairs. Hattie brushes against my hip, tail wagging like it's just another Tuesday adventure. Her confidence somehow steadies me.

"I'll put her in a bedroom while I deal with the guest," Jake says.

He opens my bedroom door and gently shuts her inside. Her one-bark protest is short-lived.

Jake looks at me, all business now. "Where exactly is it?"

"Bathroom at the end of the hall. Under the towel shelves."

"Do you think there's any way it got out?"

"No. I blocked the door with a towel. Nothing else was open."

He nods. "Okay. You stay back."

I do.

He cracks the door, peers in. Then opens it wider and steps inside, kneeling to look under the shelves.

And that's when it happens.

A black streak darts from the bathroom—right at me.

I scream. Loud. Embarrassingly loud.

Jake bolts from the bathroom, grabs the snake mid-slither with the tongs, lifting it high into the air.

It's huge. At least six feet long.

I collapse against the railing, heart pounding, chest tight, legs weak.

"You okay?" he asks.

"I cannot believe you just did that."

He grins. "Practice."

"Where are we putting it?"

He shrugs. "Outside."

"She won't come back, will she?"

"Probably not. We'll check for entry points. But she might've slipped in through an open door or crack somewhere."

We walk down the stairs, Jake holding the snake out in front of him, its long body hanging limply.

"She's fine," he says, reading my concern. "The tongs won't hurt her."

We cross the yard to the woods. Jake lowers her gently to the ground. She doesn't hesitate, just races off into the leaves.

I exhale, finally, shoulders dropping.

"How do I even begin to thank you?"

"You don't have to," he says. "I get it. Lots of people are afraid of snakes. That one was harmless, a black rat snake. But still. I wouldn't want to wake up with it next to me either."

"Please don't say that," I say, laughing despite myself. "Now I'm going to have nightmares."

"You can buy repellent, stuff that smells like peppermint oil. Supposed to keep them away."

"Where do I get it?"

"Hardware store. Or online. I can send you the link."

"Thank you. Really. Thank you, Jake."

We walk back to the house. The sun is lowering over the lake, sky softening into gold.

"You settling in okay?" he asks.

"I've been making lists," I say. "I'm getting the house ready to sell."

He pauses. "Oh. Have you found a realtor?"

"No. Not yet."

"I know someone. I can send you his number."

"Thanks," I say, hearing the note in his voice, surprise, maybe. Disappointment, too.

He watches me for a beat, then asks quietly, "Did you ever come back? After..."

I shake my head. "No. Not since—"

"Yeah," he says. "I didn't think so."

We stand there, silence settling between us, full of what we're not saying.

"I've thought about you," he says. "Your family. I wanted to reach out, but..."

"I know," I say, cutting him off gently. "Me too. It just seemed easier to leave it alone."

"Right."

But standing here now, I'm not sure that was true. Maybe we should have said more. Done more. Maybe the pain didn't have to live this long without air.

"Would you like something to drink?" I ask.

"I'm good," Jake says. He starts to turn, then stops. "Actually... I was thinking of grilling tonight. Would you want to come over?"

The invitation catches me off guard.

And for a second, just a second, something inside me lifts. The boulder shifts.

But then I remember why I'm here. What I've decided.

I can't let Jake back in. Not now. Not when I have nothing to offer. Not when I've already decided to walk away.

"Thank you," I say gently. "But I need to make some calls. Get things moving with the sale."

He nods, too quickly. "Of course. I get it."

"I'm sorry," I add. "It's not you. I just—"

"Tangled past and all that," he says, forcing a smile.

"Sort of," I say in a low voice.

He nods again. "Come on, Hattie."

We walk back to the house together. Hattie bounds down the stairs, thrilled to see me. I scratch behind her ears.

"I remember you always wanted a dog," I say.

"She's a gem," he replies. "Don't know what I'd do without her."

"She obviously adores you."

"It's mutual."

He heads for the door, then pauses. "Okay then."

He turns, hand on the knob. Then, just as quickly, he changes his mind.

"I'll send you that link," he says.

"Thanks."

He opens the truck door. Hattie jumps inside. Jake slides in beside her, starts the engine, and waves as he pulls down the driveway.

I watch him go with intense regret, wishing I could have given him another answer. But there is no other answer. I can't fight anymore. There's no will for that left inside me. Everything I had once lived for is gone: my family, my career. I am a shell of who I used to be. It's no one's fault. I'm rational enough to understand this. It's the way it is. The path my life has taken. The circumstances that conspired to take away the people I loved. And more recently, my inward collapse, stealing my ability to follow through on a career I loved as well.

I walk inside, my feet heavy as lead. The boulder settles again on my chest.

I head into the kitchen and make a cup of coffee, not because I want it, but because I need to do something. Anything.

I sit at the table, open the Notes app on my laptop, and start searching for a local painter.

One number. Then another.

I'm not getting up until I finish this list.

Because it's the only thing I have right now that still feels like I'm in control of it.

---

THE EMAIL ARRIVES JUST as I'm finishing up my list.

It's from Kate, Michael's sister. We met only once, at a

dinner that felt too polished, too quiet. She was kind. Gentle. And mostly silent.

I start reading with a pit in my stomach.

*Hi Sawyer,*

*I hope this isn't too much, or too soon. I was going through some of Michael's things this morning—just trying to sort through a few boxes. I found a letter with your name on it. It was never mailed. I don't know why. But I felt like you should know it exists. No pressure at all, but if you'd like, I can text you a photo of it. Or just send it in the mail. Let me know.*

*Warmly,*

*Kate*

I stare at the screen for a long time, heart suddenly too loud in my ears.

A letter.

From Michael.

Written, sealed, and never sent.

I reply: Please text me a photo of it.

I close my laptop and go in the bathroom to wash my face and brush my teeth, a dull knot of anxiety in my chest. My phone dings from the nightstand in the bedroom. I drop the towel in my hand and walk over to pick it up. The notification says it's from Kate. I tap the screen and open the text, then click on the photo.

I immediately recognize Michael's precise handwriting. Seeing my name in his ink makes something in my chest crack.

The letter is short. One page. No greeting, no closing. Just his voice.

*Sawyer,*

*I know I've asked a lot of you, loving someone who lives by clocks and capital markets. And I know I don't always say what you probably need to hear. But if I haven't told you lately—thank you. For showing up. For staying. For reminding me there's a world beyond the one I try to control. I don't know what our future looks like. But I know you're the only one I want in it.*

*Michael*

I read it twice.

And then I cry. Not with guilt. Not with regret. Just love for the kind, caring man he had been.

He knew something was coming.

Maybe not death. But change.

An ending. A shift.

He left me a kindness.

He left me a door I didn't know I needed to walk through.

I close my eyes and whisper a thank you.

To Michael.

To Kate.

To the woman I was then, who kept showing up. Even when she was drowning.

Some things in my life are going to be left unfinished.

But this doesn't feel like one of them anymore.

# TEN

**Jake**

FOR DINNER THAT night, I pull some things from the fridge for the grill, red peppers, onions, zucchini, squash. I slice the vegetables on a wooden cutting board, wrap them in foil, drizzle olive oil over the top, then sprinkle sea salt.

I carry the foil pouch out to the deck, fire up the grill, and place the vegetables inside.

Hattie follows me, flopping down near the railing with her chin on her paws. Her eyes drift closed.

I lean against the rail and look out at the lake. A couple of boats glide across the water, one with a skier slicing through the stillness. Another floats idly, its passengers content to watch the sunset.

And I try to make sense of what happened with Sawyer earlier today.

There's not much sense to make. The only real conclusion is the obvious one, it was a bad idea. I shouldn't have asked her to come for dinner. I don't even know what made me say it. Habit, maybe. Kindness.

Hope.

The chasm between us is twenty-five years wide, and Sawyer clearly has no interest in closing it. Not that I can blame her. Seeing me probably brings up more pain than peace. The same is true for me, if I'm honest.

Still, seeing her cracked something open. The scent of smoke and rain drifts off the lake, and suddenly I'm seventeen again.

A reminder of when I first realized that life doesn't always hand out consequences based on fairness. That sometimes bad things happen to good people. And there's no changing it—no matter how much you wish you could.

---

*That Summer*

I HAD NEVER HAD a friend like Tommy before.

He approached life with a kind of joy I'd only ever known as a little kid. Seventeen, and nothing held him back. He didn't take from others to feed that joy. It was honest. Light. Generous.

He didn't lead girls on. He made it clear when he wasn't looking for anything serious. Somehow, that level of maturity didn't come across as cold—it was just Tommy. Fun, fair, free.

I wasn't wired like that.

But I respected it.

And I liked being around it.

As for Sawyer and me, we walked a line that summer. One we both silently agreed not to cross, mostly so we could keep spending time with Tommy. We both adored him, in different ways. And I envied the relationship they had.

One late June afternoon, Tommy and I had the day off. We decided to take his parents' boat out to the Cliffs, a rock formation over the lake with a rope swing tied to a tree at the top. A local daredevil spot.

Tommy invited Cassidy Smith. I knew her from school. She was fun, flirtatious, and not looking for anything complicated. Perfect for Tommy.

I'd considered inviting someone too, but with Sawyer coming, it didn't feel right. Not for her. And not for me.

Tommy anchored the boat about twenty yards out. We swam to shore and climbed the winding path up the cliff. Tommy and Cassidy walked ahead, laughing, flirting. Sawyer walked quietly in front of me, not once glancing back. I kept my gaze on the path, deliberately avoiding her legs, her bare shoulders, the shape of her in my peripheral vision.

Things between us had changed. And I didn't know how to change them back.

At the top, we stood on the edge, looking down at the deep water below.

"Who's going first?" Tommy asked.

"Not me," Cassidy said quickly.

"You've never done it?"

She shook her head. "Heard about it, never tried it. Have you, Sawyer?"

"A few times," she said. "I can go first."

"I'll go," Tommy said. "Can't let my little sister show me up."

"Please," Sawyer replied. "I've done this more times than you."

"Still gotta protect my manhood." He grinned, then stepped off the cliff and disappeared into the water.

Cassidy shrieked, then laughed when he surfaced. "You scared me to death!"

"Come on," Tommy called. "Feels amazing!"

Cassidy followed, launching herself off the rock. She hit the water clean and popped up laughing, Tommy pulling her close and kissing her.

And then it was just me and Sawyer, standing at the edge, alone.

She looked down, meeting my gaze, direct. "Would you be shocked if I said I've thought about you kissing me like that?"

The words knocked the air from my lungs. "Sawyer—"

"I know," she said quickly, still not looking at me. "It's never going to happen. But that doesn't mean I don't think about it."

I didn't know how to respond.

"Do you?" she asked. "Ever think about it?"

"I don't want to answer that."

"Why not?"

"You know why."

"Is it because of what people would think?"

"No. It's because I don't want to do the wrong thing."

"Why is it wrong when two people like each other?"

"It's not. But the timing's wrong. And down the road, maybe it'd be different."

She finally looked at me. "Couldn't it be just between us?"

"I'd know," I said quietly. "And I wouldn't feel right."

"You wouldn't be taking advantage of me. I want it, too."

She sounded older than fifteen. Wiser.

"Will you meet me tonight?" she asked. "Ten o'clock. End of the driveway."

Then she turned and jumped—gone in a blur of motion.

We didn't talk again that afternoon. There was no chance to explain that what she wanted, I couldn't give her.

And I had no intention of showing up.

Until I did.

---

I'D JUST FINISHED PICKING up groceries for my mom. It was close to ten when I turned down the road to their house. I told myself I was just passing by. That I wouldn't stop.

But I pulled into the driveway anyway.

She wasn't there. I checked the clock—9:50. Maybe she'd changed her mind. Maybe this really was ridiculous.

I started the truck. Put it in reverse.

Then I saw her, running down the gravel drive, arms

waving, smile wide. And for a second, I wished I were someone else. Someone who could meet her halfway.

Against all better judgment, I put the truck back in park.

She climbed in, breathless. "Hey."

"Hey," I said. I couldn't stop staring at her. Couldn't speak.

"I didn't think you'd come," she said softly.

"I shouldn't have."

"Then why did you?"

I didn't answer. Just started the truck.

"Where are we going?"

"I don't know. Where do you want to go?"

"Smith Mountain. I've always wanted to go to the top at night."

"If the gate's open."

We drove with the windows down. Sawyer found a radio station, let the wind tangle her hair. The image stayed with me, burned in like something I'd want to remember years from now.

We talked. Nothing heavy. Her mom didn't let her buy junk food. My mom didn't care what I bought as long as I cooked it. She had two parents. I had one, and barely that.

Tommy had a date. We both knew that. He'd probably never imagine we were together right now.

Sawyer stuck her hands out the window, air rushing past her fingers. "You're a lot like Tommy," she said.

I shook my head. "No. You are."

She smiled, and it lit up the truck like moonlight.

"You're smarter than you think, you know."

At the top, we parked and walked out onto the overlook. I helped her up the rocks, careful to keep some space between us.

"Thank you," she said, holding onto my hand.

"I don't bite," she teased.

"I know," I said, but slipping my hand out of hers.

The lake shimmered below us, moonlight glinting off the surface like scattered glass. "Thank you," she whispered.

We sat. Talked. She asked questions, about school, football, concussions, college. About my mom. About who I thought I might be someday.

And then, the question I wasn't ready for: "When I'm older, do you think you could ever like me as more than a friend?"

I looked at her, and the weight of it sat between us.

"It wouldn't be right," I said. "Not now."

"I know," she said. "But it doesn't mean I don't think about it."

Her honesty was sharp and soft all at once. It undid me.

She asked if we could still be friends.

I told her yes.

And I meant it.

She said, "When I'm sixteen, can we talk about it again?"

I smiled, shook my head. "Then I'll be eighteen. You still won't be."

"People used to get married at sixteen," she argued.

"Things aren't like that anymore."

We stared at the lake, the world quiet around us.

"What if you meet someone else?" she asked.

"You will," I said. "Someone better."

"No. I won't. I don't want to."

Her voice was so sure, so full of belief in me, it scared me. Because deep down, I didn't believe in myself the way she did. I didn't know if I could become the man she saw in me.

But I wanted to.

So I told her the truth: "I want to be your friend, Sawyer."

She smiled softly. "I want to be yours, too."

And that night, under a sky full of stars, we were.

Just that.

Just friends. There with each other and for each other.

For then, anyway.

"Though lovers be lost, love shall not;
And death shall have no dominion."
— **Dylan Thomas, And Death Shall Have No Dominion**

# ELEVEN
## THE DAY TOMMY DIED

**Sawyer**

 I CAN STILL see it as clearly as if it happened yesterday. It was the kind of summer day we'd had a hundred times before. But the heat had a weight to it that afternoon. Heavier than usual. Like the sky was holding its breath. Sunlight flickered off the lake, bouncing against the dock like a thousand tiny mirrors. The air smelled like gasoline and sunscreen, like damp wood and hot asphalt. Boats eased in and out of their slips with a kind of lazy rhythm. Nothing urgent. Nothing unusual. I was sitting on the edge of the dock with a Dr. Pepper in my hand, my feet dangling in the water, the plastic cup dripping condensation down my leg. Tommy had just come in from a run, soaked through his shirt and still grinning. He'd already shucked his running shoes and was barefoot. He always grinned after he ran. Like it shook loose something unbelievably happy inside him. Jake was already down by the water, helping a couple tie up their ski boat.

Tommy jogged over, called out something teasing in Jake's direction, and bent forward to grab the lift wire. There was a sound, abrupt and strange. Like a crack or a pop. And then Tommy froze. His whole body seized, rigid and wrong, and then he fell onto the dock. His limbs jerked violently. A faint hiss rose from his hand, the air filling with the acrid scent of burned skin. The smell hit me, sharp and horrible. For a second, I didn't understand what I was seeing. Then the cup slipped from my fingers and hit the water, sinking. Jake shouted his name. "Tommy!" And ran flat out to reach him. The next moments came in fragments. Voices rising around us. Someone yelling to call 911. I couldn't move. I couldn't breathe. The sunlight refracted across the rippling water, turning it red and gold, and I remember thinking it looked like fire. Not blood. Fire. And still I sat there, unmoving. Then I heard my own scream, sharp and primal. Like it came from somewhere outside of me. Jake turned Tommy over on the boards and started compressions. Tommy's lips were blue. His chest was still. Jake yelled his name again and again.

Whispered please until the word cracked in his throat and broke apart. But Tommy didn't wake up. I fell to my knees beside them. Jake's arm shot out, holding me back. He didn't say anything, just shook. And cried without tears. Later, they said it was the wiring. A short in the lift. A fault no one knew was there until it was too late. Tommy had touched it barefoot, soaked in sweat, laughing. Reaching for the cable with all the ease of having done so a hundred other times. And then he was gone. Just like that. One moment, he was the sun at the center of everything, and the next moment, he was a silence none of us knew how to carry. Jake never left his side. He sat there, shaking, until the ambulance came. He didn't speak. His eyes were hollow. He'd tried to save Tommy. He did everything he could. But I saw what it did to him. How it shattered something inside him. The boy who tried to save my brother. And couldn't. I know part of him died that day. And a part of me died that day too. Not just the part that loved Tommy. But the piece of me that believed the world was safe. The piece of me that believed anything, or anyone, could be saved if you tried hard enough. It was a lesson I would learn again.

"No one ever told me that grief felt so like fear."
— **C. S. Lewis, A Grief Observed**

# TWELVE

**Sawyer**

I START CLEANING the kitchen not long after Jake drives away.

I need something to do, something to focus on that isn't the look on his face when I turned down his invitation. That flicker of hurt. The one I hadn't meant to cause but did anyway.

I didn't intend to sound cold, but I know I did. And it makes me dislike myself in new and unfamiliar ways.

I hate this version of me.

The one who recoils instead of reaches out.

The one who doesn't know how to be anything but alone.

I fill a bucket with water at the kitchen sink and add a splash of bleach I found in the laundry room. The gloves I also found there, still sealed in their original packaging, make a satisfying snap when I pull them on. I imagine my mother doing the same thing. I imagine her humming, her hands moving across these same countertops, her rhythm steady and sure.

I miss her with a pain so sharp it steals my breath.

I set the bucket on the floor, dip the rag into the water, and begin to scrub. Hard. I don't let myself think, just focus on each motion. I start with the sink. I scrub until the porcelain shines, until the chemical sting of bleach clings to the air like penance.

When I'm done, sweat drips down my spine, dampens my forehead. The sink gleams. The counters are clean. The room smells like something has been erased.

If only it were that easy.

If only we could scrub away the layers of what life leaves behind. The buildup of grief, regret, memory. The hardened film of everything we've endured, until we're new again.

Unmarked.

Untouched.

Unruined.

Another memory slips in. The summer I was hopelessly in love with Jake.

I would've taken any form of him back then, friendship, silence. I just wanted to be near him. I wonder now if he ever truly noticed me, or if I was just the awkward younger sister of his best friend. I think about the way he always treated me, with patience, gentleness. He never laughed when I asked a serious question, even when the answer was more complicated than I could understand.

Back then, I believed if I was just good enough, smart

enough, thoughtful enough, maybe he'd see me. Really see me.

Now, my cheeks burn with shame for how desperate I must have seemed. Jake never made me feel foolish.

And that was what I loved most about him.

I wonder what might have happened if Tommy hadn't died. If that summer had played out the way we imagined it might.

But there's no point in wondering.

Tommy's death rewrote everything.

Any path that might have existed between Jake and me disappeared the moment my brother reached for that cable. After that, we couldn't look at each other without seeing what was lost. Without asking the unspoken question: Could we have stopped it?

I'll never stop wondering if I could have. If I hadn't been so focused on Jake. If I'd looked sooner.

Moved faster.

Noticed.

But I didn't.

And he died.

The truth is, none of us walk away from life unweathered. The little things, the moments that don't seem like much at the time, chip away slowly. But it's the storms we don't see coming that change us. That wash out the ground beneath our feet and leave us standing on something hollow.

I've weathered a lot in my life.

But this storm, the one I've been living inside these past few months, it's the one I can't get back up from.

For the first time, I see it clearly.

I'm not going back.

Not to medicine.

Not to the version of myself who believed she could keep death at bay.

And strangely, that realization doesn't devastate me. It relieves me.

When I was in it, I didn't realize how heavy the weight was. The pressure to keep people breathing. To stand in the space between life and death and pretend you're strong enough to be okay with which way it goes.

I did my best.

I know I did.

But it wasn't enough. Not in the end.

This wasn't the kind of medicine we were trained for. This was war. No relief. No recovery.

Just a steady line of gurneys down the hallway, each one colder than the last.

It was the kind of nightmare I'd once imagined volunteering for, somewhere far away, in a war-torn village halfway around the world.

But I never signed up.

Because I knew I couldn't handle it.

And the truth is, I was right.

Except this war came to me anyway. And there was no exit. No rotation. No clean escape.

I never went back after the night I collapsed in the ER hallway. Later, I made it official, sent in my resignation. I didn't argue. I didn't cry. I just let it happen because I had nothing left to fight for.

And I was grateful. At least I didn't have to choose.

There's nothing left in me to give. No spark, no calling. I don't have the energy to figure out what comes next.

And that's why I made my choice.

It wasn't impulsive.

It wasn't dramatic.

It was quiet. Logical. Final.

One simple act. That's all it would take, peaceful, certain.

And for the first time in months, the thought doesn't scare me.

I'm not going to wake up one day and feel better.

This isn't something you come back from.

And Jake?

I can't see him again.

Because it wouldn't be fair.

To him. Or to me.

He doesn't need to carry guilt about this.

He's already carried more than his share.

# THIRTEEN

**Jake**

I DREAM ABOUT Sawyer that night.

She's at the top of an enormous outcrop of rock that looks like the Cliffs, the place we'd gone to dive from that summer we met, except this rock is much larger. It's like a mountain, and with Sawyer standing at the top, she looks miles away, so far up in the sky that I can barely see her from my spot at the base.

There's no water below, only dry ground. I call her name again and again, shouting until my throat burns, but she doesn't hear me. She's looking out into the distance, stepping closer to the edge. My heart slams against my ribs, dread rising fast and cold. I know what she's about to do. I yell her name one last time, and then I'm awake, bolting upright, sweat streaming down my face.

I sit for a moment, trying to get my bearings, and then I

realize that it's not sweat, but tears. I sit there in the dark for a couple of minutes, trying to figure out what the dream meant and why I would be dreaming such a thing. I don't let myself think about what would have happened if I hadn't woken up.

Have I picked up on something in Sawyer that my subconscious is trying to warn me about? It seems preposterous, and yet I can't deny that something about this nags at me in a way I can't turn away from. I would like to call it ridiculous and chalk it up to my current state of mind, the difficulty of these past couple of months, living in quarantine and having terror stoked with every news report, but somehow I know this isn't it. I have a gut feeling that something is wrong, and I can't give myself anything else to regret in this life.

I glance at the alarm clock on the nightstand next to the bed. It's just after five a.m. I know there's no chance I'm going back to sleep now. I get up and head for the bathroom. Hattie whines, questioning why I'm up this early. "You go back to sleep, girl," I say, but when I head downstairs to put on some coffee, she's right at my heels.

I let her out in the yard, and after I pour my cup of coffee, I walk outside barefoot to join her. We head down to the dock and watch the sun rise, and as it ascends the horizon, a pink ball in the sky, I make my decision.

If I'm wrong, Sawyer will question my sanity and forbid me from setting foot on her property again. So I come up with a way to get in front of her without making it obvious.

I gather a number of tools from my garage and load them into the back of the truck. I pull into Sawyer's driveway at just past eight. Lights are on in the house, so I'm assuming she's awake.

I get out, Hattie bounding down beside me and trotting off to explore the yard. I walk to the front door, knock and wait with my heart pounding, aware that there's every likelihood she'll turn down my offer and send me on my way.

The door opens, and Sawyer is standing there, holding a cup of coffee, surprise on her face.

"Good morning," I say.

"Good morning?" she says, a question mark at the end.

I wave a hand at my truck. "I had some extra time on my hands. I was wondering if you might want me to trim up some of the tree limbs in your yard. I noticed some of them are growing up against the house."

"Oh," she says, looking at the trees as if she's seeing them for the first time. "Yeah, I think I have that on my To-Do list. And you don't need to do that really. It's a lot of work."

"I don't mind," I say. "Like I said, I've got a few extra hours this morning, and it'd be nice just to be outside doing something productive."

"Jake," she says, and I can hear the reluctance in the utterance of my name, "I don't think it's such a good idea."

"Trimming the trees?" I say, deliberately obtuse.

"No," she says, looking at me poignantly. "You being here."

"Sawyer, I'm not looking for anything other than to help out a friend. That's it. I get it. You've got a life somewhere else."

"I did have a life," she says, dropping her gaze. It seems

like I should let her continue, but something tells me it's better to steer the conversation elsewhere.

"I've got the tools and a ladder in the back of my truck. You don't even need to be out here. I can just get started."

"I can't let you do it by yourself," she says. "I'm perfectly capable of piling up limbs. Would you like a cup of coffee?"

"Yeah," I say. "Actually, that sounds good."

"Come on, then," she says.

I glance over my shoulder to see Hattie trotting toward us. "And Hattie too, of course," she says. Hattie creeps up on the porch and wags her tail at Sawyer, dropping to a sit and waiting to have her head rubbed. Sawyer does so, almost reluctantly, as if it's been a long time since she let herself show affection for anyone or anything.

She turns then quickly, as if the connection is too much, and slips away through the foyer and into the kitchen. The house is as I remember it, the same furnishings, the same curtains. The kitchen looks a bit outdated. It's clean though, and obviously, someone has been taking care of it on a semi-regular basis at least.

Sawyer pulls a cup from the cabinet, pours coffee from the pot on the counter and says, "Do you take anything in it?"

"No. Just black." She hands me the cup, and we stand, both sipping our coffee while Hattie flops down on the linoleum floor, panting from her exuberant exploring.

"Why are you here, Jake?" Sawyer asks then, her gaze fixed on me.

"I guess I'd just like to help you out. You seem like you might be in a place where help would be a good thing."

"I appreciate that," she says, "but your day is full with your own obligations."

I lift my shoulders in a shrug. "Yeah, I can't deny that. I believe friends are important, and that we have very few in our lives that end up being the real thing. But what I remember having with you, Sawyer, was real. The timing wasn't the best, but it was real."

I watch as she processes what I've just said. Her eyes widen as the words surprise her. They aren't what she expected.

"We were so young," she says.

"We were, I agree. But that doesn't mean that friendship isn't a real thing, even at that age."

"I remember what I felt for you was more than friendship," she says, looking uncomfortable. "And I remember wishing we were at a point in life I could act on that. Did you stay that honorable?"

And I can see she wants to know. She's not being sarcastic.

"I think by my definition, I've tried. It was never my intention to do anything other than that, but maybe other people haven't seen it that way."

"What do you mean?" she asks.

"Just that sometimes people can have other motivations from what you might have assumed."

She wants to ask more, but this isn't a road I can take with Sawyer. I couldn't stand seeing the disappointment in her eyes if she knew how my life had gone.

"Where do you think we should pile up the branches?" I ask in a deliberate attempt to change the conversation.

"We could do a controlled burn at some point, so it would be nice if they were all within a spot far from the house. Is that what people typically do?"

"Yeah, it's what I did when I was cleaning up my place."

"Okay," she says. "That sounds like a plan."

I set my cup on the counter. "Thanks for the coffee."

"You're welcome." She puts her cup next to mine, and my gaze snags there. I let myself consider what it would have been like to spend my life with her, what might have happened if we'd met two years later. If we could have found a way to be together. I wonder how many mornings there would have been where we would have set our coffee cups next to each other as we headed out for our individual days. I lift my gaze abruptly back to hers and say, "Better get started."

We head for the yard on the driveway side of the house. Hattie follows, her head up high, tail wagging. She's excited to have something new to do today, and I reach down and rub under her chin.

"She's beautiful," Sawyer says.

"Thanks," I say. "I've always loved Labs. Her absolute joy for life each day is a reminder to me not to be grumpy about things I shouldn't be grumpy about. She's happy just to get up every morning and walk across the dew-soaked grass, sniffing flowers."

"People should take notes from that," Sawyer says. "Including me."

We're at the back of the truck now. I pop the tailgate,

pulling out my chainsaw and the limb clippers for the smaller branches. "Why don't you tell me, tree by tree, what you would like done, and I'll cut what we need to cut, and then we can carry the limbs to whatever spot you choose for piling them up."

"I think there's a wheelbarrow in the garage," she says.

"That would be helpful," I say. "I should have thought about that."

She walks across the yard to a side door that leads into the garage. A moment later, I hear a click and then the raising of the doors. She rolls the wheelbarrow out. It's the old-fashioned kind, metal and heavy.

"That should serve the purpose," I say. She parks it next to the first tree, and we talk for a moment about which limbs need to be taken off and how we might shape the lower limbs.

The tree we attempt is a juniper that has grown wide and tall, right up against the house. I notice that a water spigot is behind the tree, unreachable because of how close to the house the tree has grown. "Would you like to shape up the back side a bit so you could get a hose in here?"

She sticks her head around the tree to see what I'm talking about. "Yeah, that's a good idea. I didn't realize that was there."

I pick up the chainsaw, give the cord a tug. The engine makes a loud noise. I walk around the tree and set the saw against the lowest limb. I take that one off and then another nearby, step back and turn off the chainsaw.

"Think that'll give you enough room?"

"Yeah," she says. "That's a lot better." She picks up the

limbs and starts across the yard with them. And then looking back over her shoulder, "Do you think over here at the corner of the yard might be an okay place to stack everything up?"

"That should be far enough from the house. We're not planning to start a bonfire, so it should be fine." I start the saw again, shortening the limbs that have grown out too far, working until I have returned the tree to a width that seems in proportion with the house. By the time I'm finished, we have a stack of limbs which we both put into the wheelbarrow.

I roll it across the yard and add it to the pile she began with the first two limbs. We start on the second tree next, a poplar that has to be at least one hundred years old. "This is a great tree. I love poplars."

"Me too," she says. "My mom taught us how to make pocketbooks with the leaves when we were little." She picks a leaf from the limb I've just removed and says, "Did you ever learn how to make those?"

"No," I say, smiling. "Wasn't into pocketbooks."

She begins folding the sides of the leaf just so and then uses the stem to run up the center to secure them. "See?" she says, holding it up.

"It does look like a pocketbook," I say. She smiles then, and I notice that it's the first genuine smile I've seen from her since meeting up with her at Carl's. It reaches her eyes, and we lock gazes for a moment. And then she's dropping hers, and the smile disappears, as if she feels guilty for it.

I want to ask her why, but somehow I know it isn't the right time. So I start to work on the rest of the tree. We finish this one in silence. Again, carting the limbs by wheelbarrow to our ever-growing pile.

We work until noon, and by that time, we've completed all the trees in the backyard that needed the work.

My shirt sticks to my shoulder blades, sweat beading on my forehead. Sawyer has worked up a sweat as well, and once we pull the final limb to our pile, she says, "I made some tea. Would you like a glass?"

"I'd love one, with some extra ice if you don't mind."

"Come on in," she says.

"I think I'll change my shirt first. I've got an extra in the truck."

She looks at me as if she's not sure what to say, and then, "Oh, of course."

Hattie has been watching us from a nice wide strip of shade under the Poplar tree and follows me to the truck. I pull a bowl from behind my seat and pour from the bottle of water I keep there for her. She drinks, thirsty.

I grab a clean T-shirt from the passenger seat, pull off my sweaty one and put the new one on. We head for the house, and I hear Sawyer call out, "I'm in here."

I wipe my boots on the doormat and then follow the hall to the kitchen. Sawyer hands me the glass of tea, and says, "Would Hattie like some water?"

"I just gave her some, but thank you."

"Sure," she says, taking a sip of her iced tea.

I down mine in a few gulps. "That's good tea," I say.

"Mango," she says. "It's my favorite."

"That's something I've never learned how to make very well, iced tea."

"I could show you," she says. "It's not hard. You just have to use enough tea bags. I don't like it when it's too weak."

"Me either," I say. "I can come back tomorrow, and we could tackle the lakeside yard."

"You don't have to do that, Jake. It's a lot to ask of you."

"I don't mind. I would stay and do more this afternoon, but I need to do a few things to my berries."

"When will they be ripe?"

"In a couple of weeks," I say.

"That must be rewarding. Planting and seeing them grow to something beautiful and edible."

"It is," I say. "It's not something I ever imagined myself doing, but after I bought the property, and the field was there, I thought it might be nice to see what I could do with it. It's kind of addictive once you have success growing something like that. I want each year to be better than the one before it."

"What do you do with all of them?"

"I have families who come every year to pick their own berries. Most freeze them to use for pies and smoothies, or at least that's what they tell me. I don't use any chemical sprays, so everything falls under the category of organic. It doesn't make sense to me to do it any other way. Conventional farming uses chemical sprays on strawberries."

"That's never made much sense to me," she says. "Especially not as a doctor. I don't understand putting things on our food that are poisonous to anything. If it's poisonous to insects, it's poisonous to us to some degree as well."

"Yeah, that's how I see it."

"Would you like to come over this afternoon and see the field?" I ask, the invitation out before I can rethink it.

She doesn't answer me right away, struggling with the answer. Maybe she wants to, maybe she doesn't, but she says, "I should stay here and work on some of my To-Do list."

"Okay," I say. I set my glass on the counter. "Well, I guess I better get going."

"I can't thank you enough," she says. "Really, it was so nice of you."

"Don't think a thing about it, Sawyer. I was happy to do it. Come on, Hattie girl." I pat my leg, and she gets up from the floor, throwing a glance at Sawyer as if she wonders whether she's coming with us or not.

"Bye, Hattie," Sawyer says.

Hattie's tail wags, and she follows me from the house to the truck. It's not until I'm backing out of the driveway that I glance up to see Sawyer watching us from the living room window. She looks like she is sad to see us go.

"What's past is prologue."
— **William Shakespeare**

# FOURTEEN

**Sawyer**

I SPEND THE next morning cleaning out the dock house.

For some reason, I need to be outside. Focusing my energy here gives me something to do, somewhere to put all the restless weight still sitting on my chest.

The dock house is worse than I expected. Cobwebs cling to every corner. I start with the broom, knocking them down even as I feel a twinge of guilt for undoing the intricate worlds the spiders have spun.

My thoughts drift back to Jake. I keep sweeping, harder now, as if I can drive him out of my head. I try to steer the thoughts away, but they keep circling. I know I shouldn't have let him stay yesterday. Letting him help created something between us, a thread I'm not sure I can, or should, pull tighter.

Two hours in, my palms ache from gripping the broom, and my arms are sore from scrubbing the dock floor with a bucket of soapy water and a rag.

I sit on the edge of the dock, dipping my feet into the lake. It's still cold, spring hasn't fully settled in yet, but the sun is warm on my shoulders, filtered through the just-emerging canopy of leaves overhead.

A soft wind moves across the water, rippling the surface. It's the first time I've noticed a breeze since I got here.

The lake looks different in the light, no longer lifeless, but quietly awake. Like it's remembering how to breathe.

I let my eyes close, just for a moment, and listen to the rhythm of it, the wind, the water, the birdsong returning after winter. And something inside me... loosens.

Then I stand and wander to the back corner of the dock house, the last section I haven't touched yet.

It's cluttered with gear. A deflated inner tube. A half-broken paddle. Coiled rope stiff with age.

I reach behind a leaning wooden oar and pause.

Propped against the wall, half-hidden beneath an old tarp, is a single water ski.

Faded blue. UVA sticker curling at the edges.

I know it instantly.

Tommy's.

I pull it out carefully, brushing away a fine layer of dust. The bindings are worn, the surface sun-bleached and scratched. But it's here.

Somehow, after all these years, it's still here.

I sit down slowly, cradling it in my lap. My fingers trace

the shallow grooves along the edge, grooves he carved himself when we were teenagers. He called them "battle scars." Swore they made the ski faster. I'd rolled my eyes but believed him anyway. Because when Tommy said something, I believed him. Always.

A tear slips down my cheek before I can stop it.

The ache is still there, sharp as ever, but it doesn't hollow me out the way it used to. It hurts, but it doesn't take everything with it.

It's strange how grief can wait in silence. How it hides in forgotten places and finds you when you least expect it.

I stand and lean the ski gently against the dock wall, upright, in view. Not hidden anymore.

He's gone.

But he was here.

And part of him still is.

"Let yourself be silently drawn by the stronger
pull of what you truly love."
— **Rumi**

# FIFTEEN

**Sawyer**

I'M SITTING ON the deck later that evening, thinking about what Jake said.

I still have no appetite. I'm too tired to cook. Maybe still too numb to want anything at all. I sip a glass of white wine, chilled and dry, and set it down on the rail, blinking into the yard where something moves near the edge of the trees.

At first, I think it's a dog, skinny, with sharp angles and an alert posture. It sits on its haunches, facing me. The light is dim, but I have the strange sensation it's watching me. I don't move, afraid to startle it. Afraid it will vanish before I can make sense of its presence.

Slowly, as my eyes adjust, I realize it's not a dog at all.

It's a coyote.

A twinge of unease coils in my chest, but it fades quickly.

After everything I've seen, everything I've lived through, this doesn't feel like fear. Not real fear. Not the kind that changes you.

He stays there. Still. Focused. Thin. Maybe old. Maybe lost.

And suddenly, I feel something strange. Like I recognize him. Or maybe I just understand him. Alone. Unsure of where to go. Looking for something he probably won't find.

Without letting myself overthink it, I pull out my phone and call Jake. Reaching for someone feels foreign... but it doesn't feel wrong. Not tonight.

"Hey," I say.

"Hey. Everything okay?"

"I think there's a coyote in my yard."

A pause. "Are you all right?"

"I'm fine. He's not close. But he's been sitting there for a while. Watching me. He looks like he might be hungry."

"I wouldn't go near him. Want me to come check it out?"

"You don't have to. I just didn't remember them being around here."

"They weren't, not years ago. But lately, yeah. There's been a lot of clear cutting in the area. They've lost habitat."

"That's sad."

"It is. They're incredibly adaptable. They eat everything, bugs, crops, dog food, even watermelon. They've survived because they're hard to get rid of. But there aren't sanctuaries or places that will help them. They're considered a nuisance species."

"That's awful. So I should just leave him alone?"

"Yeah. That's the best thing you can do. But I doubt you will."

There's silence on the line. And then, without fully knowing why, I say, "No. I won't. I'll put some food out for him."

"I'd do the same."

And I know he would. "Okay." I hesitate, and then, "Do you want to come over for a drink?"

"I'll be there in a few minutes."

---

WHEN JAKE PULLS into the drive, I've already put some sliced turkey out for the coyote. He ate it and then melted into the woods like he was never there at all. I wonder if he'll be back.

Jake knocks, and I open the door. We walk through the foyer and into the kitchen.

"Do you want a glass of wine?" I ask.

"Honestly? I'd rather have a beer, but—"

"I don't have any."

"Wine it is, then."

I pour him a glass, and we carry it outside. He leans against the deck railing, swirling the wine before taking a sip.

"Pretty good," he says. "Not that I know much about wine."

"It was here. Left in a cabinet. I was surprised the cork hadn't crumbled."

We both watch the dark where the coyote had been.

"Gone?" Jake asks.

"Yes. He left when you pulled in."

"Not surprising. They don't hang around long once they know they've been seen."

"It was strange, though. He didn't seem afraid of me. It was like he was trying to tell me something."

Jake turns slightly toward me. "I get that. Living out here, I've felt it too. A kind of understanding between us and the animals. Like we're sharing space that doesn't really belong to either of us."

I nod. "This house. The land. It all feels temporary now. When I was younger, it felt like forever. Like if we owned something, we'd outlast it. But that's never really true, is it?"

"No," Jake says quietly. "I think it's not about how long we're here. It's about what we do with the time we are."

I glance at him, startled by how much that echoes what I've been struggling to name. "I used to think I had that part figured out. My job, my purpose. It all made sense, until it didn't."

"Will you go back?" he asks gently.

"No," I say without hesitation. "I can't. I used to feel alive doing that work. Now it just feels... broken. Like I was fooling myself all along."

Jake reaches out and puts a hand on my shoulder. "No one would have tried harder than you."

The words hit something deep. I look away, biting the inside of my cheek.

"I didn't sign up for a war, Jake. But that's what it

became. Except the enemy was invisible. And relentless. And it always won. I left. I couldn't take it anymore. I couldn't keep watching people die."

"Sometimes, we do everything we can, and it's still not enough. That doesn't mean we failed."

"But what if there is no next?" I whisper. "What if I'm just... done?"

Jake is quiet for a moment. Then, "Sometimes the hardest part is waiting for the next thing to show up. We expect it to arrive right away, but it rarely does."

I glance at him. "How do you know that?"

He takes a slow sip of wine. "Have you ever looked me up online?"

I blink. "No. I thought about it. But maybe I didn't want to know what happened to you. Maybe I wanted to remember you as you were."

Jake studies me, then, after a long pause, says softly, "You could. If you want. And then I'll tell you everything. Tomorrow. Just know it might change how you see me."

I nod slowly, unsettled by his tone. There's something in it I don't recognize. Something heavier than he's let me see before.

He finishes his wine and sets the glass on the railing. "Thanks for the drink. If you see the coyote again, give me a call."

"I will. And... thank you. For coming over."

"Goodnight, Sawyer."

I stand at the door and watch him walk to his truck. I

listen to the engine hum as it rolls down the driveway. The house feels hollow once he's gone. Like something real just left it.

Inside, I set my glass in the sink and rummage for something to eat. My stomach growls, surprising me. I haven't felt hunger in days, but I make crackers with peanut butter and eat them standing at the counter.

It tastes like nourishment.

Like life.

Like maybe I'm not as far gone as I thought.

Later, in bed, I glance at the laptop. Jake's challenge lingers in my mind.

I sit down, prop pillows behind me, and type his name into the search bar.

What I find shocks me.

The headlines. The articles. The accusation. The resignation. The swirl of speculation.

There are no facts. No confirmations. Just noise. But I know what damage it can do.

As a doctor, I've seen careers destroyed over accusations. I've seen people leave medicine not because they failed, but because they couldn't afford the cost of defending themselves.

Jake was never a quitter. But now I wonder what he was protecting. Who he was trying to spare.

The Jake I knew... the Jake I saw today... he doesn't match the picture painted in those stories.

I close the laptop and sit in silence. The house is still.

The truth is, I want to ask him.

Not because I'm nosy.

But because I need to believe something can still be true in a world where so much feels like a lie.

And maybe, just maybe, he's the one who can help me believe again.

# SIXTEEN

**Jake**

THE ALARM CLOCK clatters to life with its usual overzealous cheer, dragging me out of sleep. I cross the room and smack the off button, groaning as I do.

I've always had a love-hate relationship with that thing. I like early mornings, the quiet, the productivity, but some days, the interruption feels more cruel than helpful.

I shower, shave, and get dressed, and as soon as I step back into the bedroom, Hattie jumps down from the bed. She always waits until I'm ready before she gets out of bed.

We make our way to the kitchen, and I let her out into the yard while I start the coffee. She's scratching at the door before I've taken my first sip.

I let her in, and she pads straight to her food bowl, tail wagging in anticipation.

"Okay, okay," I say. "Can I get a few sips in?"

Her tail thumps the floor with polite insistence.

I take a long pull from my mug and get to work on her breakfast.

I stopped buying commercial dog food years ago, after reading too much about what actually goes into some of it. The rendering plants, the "meat byproduct" labels that could mean anything from roadkill to euthanized animals, it turned my stomach. I couldn't support that industry. Not for Hattie. Not for anyone's animal.

So I started cooking her meals myself.

Chicken with green beans, carrots, small potatoes, and brown rice. I prep a few days at a time. She thinks I'm a five-star chef, and honestly, I don't hate the praise.

This morning is no different. I warm the broth, pour it over her food, and set the bowl down. She eats like it's a feast prepared just for her, which, I guess, it is.

"If only people were as easy to please," I say.

She wags her tail but doesn't look up, too busy licking the bowl clean.

I take my coffee out onto the deck. The morning is cool, the air just damp enough to smell like soil and dew. The sun is rising pink over the lake, a soft ball of color edging up above the trees.

And I feel... grateful.

Not in the abstract sense, but grounded. Present. Aware that this place I get to live in is more than I deserve.

But there's something else this morning.

Something more than just the sunrise or the quiet.

It's the thought of Sawyer—just down the road.

I've thought about her so many times over the years. Always with the same ache, the same certainty that she was out of reach. Not just in miles, but in the way time and tragedy carve out distances we can't always close.

But now she's here. And though I know she doesn't plan to stay, just knowing she's nearby stirs something I hadn't felt in a long time.

Hope. Maybe. Or memory.

She's not the same girl I knew. I can see that. I can feel the heaviness in her, the weight of things that haven't let her go. But there's still something in her, the same pulse of quiet strength. The same hunger for truth. I wonder if being here, in this place that once brought her joy, might start to heal the fractures she thinks will never mend.

Maybe I'm fooling myself. Arrogant enough to believe I know what she needs.

But when you've known someone when they were young, really known them, you remember who they are at their very foundation. And I once knew Sawyer to be someone who believed fiercely in the good in this world. In its ability to overcome the bad.

I take another sip of coffee and wonder if I still believe that too.

I think I do.

I've lived long enough to know that pain is part of the deal. There's no clean path through a human life. We all get knocked down. We all lose people. We all come apart in our own quiet ways.

But there are also moments of peace. Beauty. Grace.

I've found them here, on this land, in the slow rhythm of tending to the things that grow.

It's not the life I once imagined.

But in many ways, it's better.

And then my thoughts return to Sawyer.

Did she look me up?

I'm guessing she did. Not out of doubt or suspicion, but out of need. Need to know if the person she once believed in was still real.

A stab of fear rises in me.

Because if she did read the stories, there's every chance she might believe them.

And if she does...

Then I'll know I was wrong about what we shared.

And that's what scares me the most.

Not the stories.

Not the fallout.

But the possibility that I was wrong about what I felt between us all those years ago.

"I can be changed by what happens to me.
But I refuse to be reduced by it."
— **Maya Angelou, Letter to My Daughter**

# SEVENTEEN

**Jake**

I'M OUT IN the field, pulling weeds with Hattie, when a vehicle comes up the driveway. I hear a door opening and then closing. Several seconds later, Sawyer appears around the corner of my tool shed.

"Hey," she says.

"Morning."

"I hope you don't mind me coming over without—"

"I never mind, Sawyer. Come on out here and help me pull some weeds."

She looks relieved, walking across the grass to join Hattie and me in a strawberry row. "There aren't that many," I say. "Just these that pop up right around the vines. The black paper keeps almost everything else from growing up, but I like to pull any I see just because I feel like they take energy away from the plant."

"That makes sense," she says. "Where should I start?"

"Anywhere you like," I say.

She walks ahead of me, Hattie by her side, tail wagging hard. Sawyer rubs her head, once, twice, three times, and then drops onto her knees and begins pulling weeds from the base of a plant. We work like that for a while in silence.

I figure when she's ready to tell me why she's here, she'll do so. And it's not long before the questions come.

"How did you live through all of that, Jake?"

I consider my answer, wanting to be accurate. "It wasn't easy," I admit. "Not for a long time, actually. I got on board the pity party boat, drank myself into more hangovers than I care to admit and despaired of ever figuring out what I was going to do with my life. I started with getting a dog, Hattie, something I'd always wanted, but never felt like I had the time for before. That turned out to be one of the best decisions I've ever made. She kind of let me see that I must not be such a bad person if she could have such a high opinion of me."

Sawyer smiles at this, searches out another weed and gives it a hard yank.

"May I ask you something?" she says without looking at me, keeping her gaze on the task at hand.

"Sure," I say.

"Was there any truth at all to the accusation?"

Coming from anyone else, I might take the question as an insult. But coming from Sawyer, that's not it. There's something in her voice that tells me she needs to know if I'm who she's always thought I was, or if I might turn out to be just another one of life's disappointments. I think about my answer, giving it the pause it deserves.

When I speak, my voice is low and even. "It's true that I should have picked up on what was happening before I did. I knew she was stopping by my office on a regular basis, but she did have some difficulty with the class I was teaching, and she told me she wanted to make a good grade to prove to her parents she was taking school seriously. That went on for six weeks or so. Until one afternoon, when she came by the office after a quiz to see if I had graded hers yet. She kissed me, and I guess I was so surprised that I didn't know what to say for a moment. But the look on my face must have told her what I was thinking, and she left the office before I could say anything. I decided to pretend it hadn't happened, thinking that would save her the embarrassment of talking about it with me. But then, the next day, she started posting stuff on social media, telling her friends not to take any of my classes because I had tried to assault her in my office. Honestly, I thought it was a joke. I didn't know whether to keep silent or attempt to address it. As you can guess, it didn't go away. It took on a life of its own, students sharing her post, until it went viral, and the truth didn't matter. I got an attorney that same day because I had a feeling that things were going to get worse. And, of course, they did. What I figured out was that it didn't matter whether I was guilty or not. All that seems to matter these days is doubt. If there's any doubt about your reputation or something you've been accused of, that's enough to turn your life upside down."

Sawyer is standing now, looking at me. I see the empathy in her eyes, feel it emanating from her like waves washing in from the ocean.

"I'm so sorry that happened to you, Jake," she says. "It's terrible. More than terrible."

"It was. But I don't question it now. I guess I've come to believe that things happen to us for a reason. And if that hadn't happened, I wouldn't be here." I consider my next words, wonder if I will come to regret them, but say them anyway. "If that hadn't happened to me, I might never have seen you again."

Surprise registers in her eyes, immediately followed by something I'm less inclined to interpret.

"I'd like to see life like that," she says. "I'm having trouble doing that, though. Maybe that's something I can learn from you."

"How to make lemonade out of lemons?"

"I don't know how you were able to do it."

"I didn't want to live my life marinating in bitterness over something I couldn't change. I grew up watching my mom do just that, and at some point, it seemed like a terrible waste of life. I didn't want to give someone else the power to do that to me. I always wondered why she couldn't reject the label she thought my dad had put on her, acknowledge it as his shortcoming and not hers."

"It's not easy to raise children alone," Sawyer says. "Not now. And not then, either."

"No, it isn't," I acknowledge. "And I always admired my

mother for having the courage to make the decision she did. She certainly could have made another one. But I always felt like she could see herself through the lens of his rejection and never opened herself up to letting someone else give her another interpretation."

"That's painful," Sawyer says.

"Yeah, it is," I agree.

"Does your mom still live here?" Sawyer asks.

"She's in a care facility in Roanoke," I say, in as even a voice as I can manage. "She has dementia."

"I'm so sorry," Sawyer says.

"I considered bringing her here to stay with me," I say, "but she had a stroke. And for now, at least, she's getting the care that she needs."

"I'm so sorry, Jake. That's an excruciating decision to have to make."

I put my attention on a particularly deep-rooted weed. "We think we have all the time in the world to fix the things in our lives that need fixing. And then, one day, we wake up and realize that we don't have that kind of time at all. In my case, I let too much of it go past without saying things that I wish I had gotten around to saying to my mom. I lived too many years focused on the things I thought she neglected to do for me, instead of realizing all the things she did right. And there were plenty. I know that now, as an adult who's had to figure out how to make it in the world. It's not an easy thing. And certainly not for someone who started out as my mom did, with a baby and no one to help support her."

"You can still say those things to her, Jake. She may not hear you as she once would have, but some part of her will know."

"You believe that?"

She looks up at me then, meets my questioning gaze with sincerity in her eyes. "I do."

"I'd like to."

"You need to say the things you need to say, Jake. For her, but for you as well. She's still here. That's what matters. There are so many things I wish I'd said to my parents that I'll never have the chance to now. Regret is an awful pill to swallow."

The sun has moved higher in the sky, and Sawyer wipes the back of her hand across her forehead. "It's gotten warm out here," she says.

"Yeah, it has. How about a glass of water?"

"Sounds good," she says.

"Come on. I'll fix us both one."

We walk through the field to the grass that leads to the house. Hattie follows us, tail wagging lazily. We take the stairs to the deck and step through the French doors of the kitchen.

"Do you mind if I wash my hands?" Sawyer asks.

"Of course not. The guest bathroom is just down the hallway there."

"Thank you."

She disappears from the kitchen, and I pull a couple of glasses from the cabinet, fill them with ice and then with water. When she returns a minute later, I hand one to her. She takes the glass with both hands, like she's steadying herself, but there's something quieter in her face than yesterday. Not ease, exactly. Just... less fear.

"Thank you so much. That looks wonderful. Your house is beautiful. Did you do any of this?" she asks, waving a hand at the decor of the kitchen.

"Yeah. Actually, I kind of did a complete renovation of the place. It needed an update, and I needed somewhere to put my focus."

"You did a great job," she says. "I love the colors, and the cabinetry is beautiful."

"Thanks," I say. "Have you thought about keeping your parents' place?"

"No," she says, shaking her head and glancing down. "I haven't."

"You could, you know. It's a good place to live. I mean, I think it's a good place."

"It's okay, Jake. I know what you meant."

She walks over to the glass-paned doors that look out across the lake, stands there, silent, before saying, "How are you not angry about what happened to you, Jake?" She turns to look at me then. "I mean, you essentially had your life as you knew it taken away from you."

"I was, for a while," I say. "I'm not going to deny that."

"What changed?"

I don't need to think about my answer. I remember the exact moment. "I came across this interview with a psychiatrist, a Holocaust survivor. She was in her late eighties at the time but full of life and purpose. She talked about being sent to Auschwitz with her mother and sister, about how the guards separated them on arrival, promising they'd be reunited soon. Her mother was gone that same day."

Sawyer watches me, barely breathing.

"Listening to her talk about finding a way to go on after something like that... it made me see what happened to me differently. Just more clearly. Made me realize that maybe everything wasn't ruined. Maybe I could still make something of what was left."

Sawyer's eyes darken and become liquid, tears falling, one by one, down her cheeks. I don't think about what I'm doing. I just cross the room and pull her into my arms, wrapping myself around her with a desire to give her what she needs in this moment, complete understanding of her pain. Her shoulders shake against my chest. I rub her hair, not offering any words of comfort, just the silent communication that I'm here for her, that on some level, as best I can, I do understand where she is and what she is feeling. I know better than to question the place she has found herself in. I know the only person who can decide to leave it is Sawyer herself. And then she slips her arms around my waist, hugging me tightly, as if she might absorb her body into mine.

We stand there, and that's okay with me, because I would be content to hold her like this forever, to be the one from whom she seeks refuge and comfort. When she pulls back and looks up at me, I see something in her I haven't seen yet. I could be wrong. Maybe I am, but I swear there's a glimmer of hope there.

After Sawyer leaves, I stand in the kitchen with my coffee cooling in my hand.

The house is quiet. Too quiet.

I set the mug down and lean against the counter, hands braced on the edge like I'm trying to keep the world from tilting again.

It's been years, but there are still days when I miss it—the classroom. The cadence of my lectures. The way a student's face would light up when something clicked. The sense that I was doing something that mattered.

There are nights I still dream about it. About the last lecture I never got to finish. The hallway I never walked again.

Some mornings, I wake up half-expecting to pack my briefcase and drive to campus.

Then I remember.

And the shame comes, quiet and heavy.

I lost everything because someone told a story louder than I could tell the truth. And I've told myself I made peace with it.

But sometimes I still wonder who I'd be now if that hadn't happened.

If I would have been stronger.

If I would have fought harder.

The truth is, I didn't want to spend the rest of my life explaining myself.

So I disappeared.

And maybe that's what hurts most.

Not the loss of my job.

But the loss of my voice.

I grip the counter a little harder.

Then Hattie pads into the room, sits by my side, and rests her head against my leg like she's reminding me of what I still have. Of what I've built. Of who I've become.

And slowly, the tightness in my chest loosens.

"The mountain you carry is teaching you how to climb."
— **Najwa Zebian, Mind Platter**

# EIGHTEEN

**Sawyer**

I'M EXHAUSTED, but not in the collapsing way. Just tired. It feels almost strange to end a day without falling apart.

I have a dream that night, as real as any I've ever had.

I'm alone in the wilderness, someplace unfamiliar, vast, and quiet, when a mountain appears in front of me. Towering. Impossible. I'm barefoot, without gear or direction, and yet I know with complete certainty: I need to climb it.

I move toward the base, but every time I do, the mountain shifts, and the center realigns. No matter where I approach, it keeps moving away from me.

Eventually, I stop trying to outmaneuver it.

And I just start climbing.

The slope is steep from the first step. I scramble upward, gripping rocks, digging my toes into shallow holds. When I finally make progress, the incline tilts again, steeper still, the top disappearing into the clouds.

But I don't stop.

I don't look up.

I just keep going.

One ledge at a time. One breath at a time. The air thins, burning my lungs, but I keep climbing.

I wake in the middle of the climb, chest heaving, soaked in sweat. My body is still, but it feels like I've been moving for hours. The sun is just beginning to creep through the curtains, the light faint and golden across the ceiling.

I lie there for a long moment, staring up, thinking about the dream.

The woman climbing that mountain—that was the old me. The girl who believed obstacles were just puzzles waiting to be solved. The one who thought endurance would always be enough.

Not that long ago, driving down here from New York, I believed she was gone for good.

That I'd never know her again.

But now... I'm not so sure.

Maybe she's still in there.

Buried, yes. Bruised, maybe.

But not gone.

Yesterday, standing in Jake's arms, I felt something stir. A quiet resolve. A flicker of fight. For the first time in weeks, maybe months, I didn't feel like someone fading.

Listening to him talk about what he'd lived through, what he'd lost, and how he kept going...

It made something inside me sit up and listen.

I realized: I can't be a victim.

I can't let life break me.

That's not who I am. That's never been who I am.

I've always wanted to give the best of myself.

To make a difference where I could.

And maybe, just maybe, that's still possible.

I don't know yet.

But for the first time in a long time, I want to find out. And the only way to do that...is to try.

"We shall not cease from exploration,
And the end of all our exploring
Will be to arrive where we started
And know the place for the first time."
— **T. S. Eliot, "Little Gidding"**

# NINETEEN

**Sawyer**

IT'S JUST AFTER eleven when I pull into Jake's driveway.

I cut the engine but don't get out right away. I sit there, staring at the front porch, wondering if this was a mistake.

But then the door opens, and Hattie bounds out, tail wagging. Jake follows, smiling.

I climb out of the Jeep and rub Hattie's back. "Hey."

"Hey," Jake says. "I thought you might've changed your mind."

"I almost did."

"I'm glad you didn't." He nods toward the lake. "Come on."

"So tell me about this plan of yours," I say as we walk across the grass.

"The best way to hike Smith Mountain is to take the Sea-

Doo across the lake and beach it at the base. Then we hike from there."

"Have you done it before?"

"Plenty," he says. "Hattie's practically the trail guide. She keeps an eye out for snakes."

"Snakes?" I repeat, not hiding my alarm.

He grins. "We probably won't see any. But yeah, copperheads, rattlesnakes... they're around. I'll lead the way."

"I could rent us a helicopter, you know," I offer. "Have us lowered onto the top."

Jake laughs. "It's the climb that makes you strong, not the view from the top."

I hadn't told him why I really wanted to do this. I hadn't mentioned the dream. Just texted him this morning to see if he was free.

Now I wonder if I was crazy.

At the dock, he hands me a slim life jacket and puts a bright pink one on Hattie.

"She can swim like a fish," he says, "but I like her to wear one when we're in deep water. Just in case."

"She looks adorable."

"Pink suits her," he says with a smile. He slips into a black life jacket, starts the engine, and motions for me to climb on. "You next. Hattie'll ride up front with me."

I get on, settle behind him, and watch as Hattie climbs on like a seasoned pro.

Jake lowers the Sea-Doo into the water and idles away from the dock. I grab the strap at the back of his vest, unsure where else to hold on. When he accelerates, I instinctively wrap my hands around his sides.

The lake stretches out, deep blue and wide beneath a clear sky. A pontoon boat drifts to our left, a wake-surfer carves waves to our right, music blaring from onboard speakers.

Jake navigates toward the open water. Hattie lifts her nose to the sky, ears flapping in the wind. She looks like pure joy.

Ten minutes later, we slow near a sandy stretch at the base of Smith Mountain.

"This place is beautiful," I say.

"It really is," Jake agrees. "I've been to Lake Como, and yeah, it's stunning, but Smith Mountain has its own kind of magic."

He guns the engine just enough to push us onto the beach, then cuts it. Hattie leaps off and takes off down the shoreline to sniff.

"Ladies first," Jake says, motioning for me to climb off. He follows, then pulls our bags from the storage compartment.

I'm wearing shorts, hiking boots, and a small backpack. Jake has a bigger one slung over his.

"The water's still cold," I say, testing it with my toe.

"It won't warm up until June. I usually swim by April, but with a wetsuit."

We sit and lace up our boots. I catch myself noticing how strong his legs are, athletic, solid.

"What do you do to stay in shape?" I ask.

"I run. Mostly trail runs. Clears my head. How about you?"

"Not much lately. This might be a wake-up call."

"You'll make it," he says, standing and adjusting his pack.

A small part of me wants to tell him I'm not sure. But another part, faint, but alive, wants to try anyway.

He leads the way to the trail. Hattie bounds ahead, tail high.

"How about I go first," Jake says. "Just in case we do meet a snake."

"Yes, please."

"You know I'm never letting you live that down, right?"

I roll my eyes. "I had a feeling."

I smile then. It feels strange. A lightness pressing up against the weight of so much darkness. But I let it come. And it feels good. Like the first rays of sun at dawn.

The climb starts steep. I follow him step by step, already regretting my severely lagging fitness level.

"You good?" he calls back.

"Still with you."

The trail zigzags through underbrush and trees. After twenty minutes, we pause on a rocky outcrop. Jake pulls out a bottle of water for Hattie, who laps it up gratefully. Then he hands me one.

"Thanks," I say, drinking deeply.

"Did you ever hike this mountain growing up?"

"No," I say. "We talked about it, but never did. I know Tommy would've loved it."

"Yeah," Jake says, brushing something invisible from his shorts. "He would have."

"It's okay to talk about him," I say gently. "I miss talking about him."

Jake nods slowly. "I don't know why it makes me feel so guilty. But it does."

"My mom never got over it," I say. "And I understand. Losing a child..." I pause. "It rewrites everything."

"Your parents created that scholarship in his name, right?"

"They did. There was a settlement. They didn't want money to be the end of his story."

"They were good people," Jake says quietly.

"They were. It's nice to talk about them with someone who knew them."

We sit in the sun a while longer. It filters through the trees in golden shards. Then Jake says, "Why did you move to New York?"

I take a moment. "I don't know. Maybe guilt. Maybe I needed to become someone else. I think I was trying to run from the old me."

"I liked the old you," Jake says, his voice low.

I glance at him. Our eyes meet and hold. I don't look away.

"Did you feel at home there?" he asks.

"No," I admit. "Not even a little. But I stayed. Almost ten years."

"That's a long time to stay somewhere that doesn't feel like home."

"It is," I say. "I got caught up in the work. The pace. The routine. I stopped asking myself if I liked it."

"Are you glad you left?"

"I wish it had happened differently. But now that I'm gone, I wonder how I lasted so long."

Jake nods. "City life never suited me. Nature's what helps me stay centered."

"It's easy to forget the world's chaos out here."

"Exactly. But I think that's part of the problem, how much noise we let in. The news. Social media. It's designed to keep us anxious."

"They know we'll stick around for the next crisis."

"It's no wonder people forget how to breathe."

"I've been guilty of that," I say. "Forgetting to be here, in the only moment we actually have."

Jake looks at me sharply, concern flashing in his eyes. I want to reassure him. I want to say I'm fine.

But I don't.

Because I don't know if I am.

I hop down from the rock. "We better keep going if we're going to make the top."

Jake rises and slings the backpack over his shoulders. "Let's go then."

We climb in silence. Hattie moves beside him, still energized. I follow, steady, even as the silence stretches.

Eventually, Jake hands me another bottle of water. We drink. Take a rest. Walk some more.

After nearly an hour, we reach the top. Hattie plops down and stretches out, panting.

The view is breathtaking.

The lake sprawls out below us, its waters silver and endless. Docks look like toothpicks. Houses like dollhouses. In the distance, a field glows green, horses grazing like flecks of shadow. For the first time in a long time, the beauty doesn't feel like something happening far away from me. I actually feel present inside it.

Jake offers his hand as I scramble over a final outcrop. I take it, and for a moment, I'm pressed against his chest.

Something shifts.

I don't know what.

But it feels important.

He brushes the back of his hand across my cheek, then slips his arm around my shoulders and turns me toward the lake.

"It's like looking down from heaven," I whisper.

"Yeah," he says. "It is."

We stand there, quiet, taking it in. Then he looks at me, steady, unguarded. I feel the pull between us, the quiet knowing that he sees me and accepts me completely. Even the cracks in my foundation. The failures. The uncertainties. And I'm grateful, so deeply grateful, to be seen as I am.

"Is it okay if I kiss you, Sawyer?"

I place my hand on his chest, feeling the warm strength of him. I nod once, hear myself whisper, "It's more than okay."

He takes his time with it, studying my face with an intensity that stirs emotion deep inside me and makes it impossible to look anywhere else. And suddenly, I realize I have been waiting for this my entire adult life. Wanting to be wanted by this man who snagged my heart as a boy a long, long time ago.

He leans in, cupping my jaw as though I might vanish if he isn't careful. He settles his mouth against mine, a whisper of a kiss, but it's enough to unravel me. Heat sparks through, so swift and consuming my knees nearly give way.

I sink into him, my fingers anchoring in his shirt. The kiss deepens, still tender but no longer careful, like a promise breaking open after years of being locked up. The air around us disappears, the only sound a flock of geese flying over the lake below us.

There's no mistaking it now. This isn't a moment borrowed from the past. It's something new, something that carries both memory and possibility, as if all the years between then and now have been leading us here.

And I know this: being kissed by Jake is everything I imagined and more.

When he pulls back, he brushes the back of his hand across my cheek.

I look up at him, not even trying to hide what I'm feeling. I don't think I could if I wanted to. "Do you believe people are meant to meet again, Jake?"

"I do now," he says, his voice low and intimate.

"I never thought I'd see you again. And yet... I think it wasn't meant to happen until now," I say, hoping he hears the truth in my voice.

He reaches out, touches my face. "Yeah," he says. "I believe that. And I also believe we weren't finished. What we had back then... it never left. Not for me."

"Not for me either," I say, the admission out before I can think better of it. "When I got here, I didn't want to keep going. I couldn't see anything good ahead. But maybe there's still something left. Maybe I'm meant to find out what it is."

Jake looks at me, eyes full of quiet emotion. "I don't know what comes next. But I'm grateful. And if you choose to stay..."

He lets the words hang, layered with meaning.

A part of me wants to retreat, afraid of wanting anything at all. But another part, small but steady, stays open. Just open. And for now, that feels like enough.

I reach out and cover his hand with mine. Squeeze once.

Words aren't necessary.

Possibility is enough for now. And for me, a reason to go on.

# TWENTY

**Sawyer**

WE GET BACK to Jake's just as the late afternoon light begins to slant across the lake. There's an ease between us, a lightness that hasn't existed until now. As if some important things had been laid open, and the unspoken questions that needed answers had finally been put to rest.

Jake fires up the grill on the deck, laying out salmon fillets with a drizzle of olive oil and lemon. I chop vegetables for a salad, the simple rhythm of cooking with another person something I hadn't realized I missed. We open a bottle of red wine and let the conversation wander, half laughter, half quiet reflection, as if we've been doing this for years instead of this single night of undeniably renewed attraction.

Music drifts through the outdoor speakers, a mellow backdrop to the evening. By the time darkness settles, we're tucked into the deep chairs on his deck, glasses of red wine in hand, watching the surface of the lake turn silver under the moonlight.

A song from our youth comes on the outdoor speakers, the melody so familiar it pulls me straight back to a time when the world felt unshakable and certain.

Jake sets his glass down, turns to me with a smile. "Dance with me?" he asks softly.

I hesitate only a second before standing and slipping my hand into his. He pulls me from my chair and draws me close. We move together to the music, slow and unhurried. The night air is cool, the scent of the grill still lingering, the world outside the two of us fading away.

At some point he pulls back just enough to touch the side of my face, his thumb brushing my cheek. His eyes hold mine, filled with a longing I feel mirrored in my own heart. He lowers his head, and when his mouth meets mine, there's no hesitation.

I kiss him back, the years between us dissolving in the press of lips, in the way our bodies lean instinctively closer. Desire hums low and sure between us.

When he finally lifts his head, his voice is rough with meaning. "Would you like to stay the night?"

It's not something I have to think about. "Yes," I say. "Yes."

He takes my hand, leading me inside, down the hallway to his bedroom. When he closes the door behind us, the quiet that follows feels like we're standing at the edge of something reverent and intimate, something we've been waiting our whole life for.

His bedroom is masculine and appealing with oversized leather chairs and a large bed with a distressed wood frame and headboard. There's warm, low lighting from bedside lamps, and I can smell the faint scent of cedar and lake air through a partially open window.

Jake turns to me, brushing a strand of hair from my face, his touch tender but charged with intent.

"Are you sure, Sawyer?" he asks, his voice low and rough with emotion.

"Yes," I whisper. The word comes automatically, steady as truth. "I'm absolutely sure."

His mouth finds mine again, unhurried at first, then deepening with every breath.

I sink into him, hands sliding over the solid warmth of his back, years of longing collapsing into this moment.

We move together as if we've known all along how we would fit. He draws me closer, his fingers splayed against my spine, and the world outside this room slips away.

He eases me back onto the bed, our kisses trailing into something slower, sweeter, and yet edged with need. His hands move with reverence, mapping the familiar and the new, reminding me of who we were and showing me who we are now.

I touch his face, memorizing the lines time has drawn there, the strength and gentleness that live side by side in him. "Jake." His name is a soft sigh on my lips, and the way he looks at me in that moment makes me realize that every year we've waited to reach this night has been worth it. I want nothing more than to give myself fully to him, to know him in the way I could only once imagine.

"I love you, Jake," I say, not wanting to hide it from him anymore. I know by any normal measuring stick, it's too soon to say it. Except that I've really always loved him. And the world no longer operates by what I once thought normal. I just want him to know it. Life is too uncertain to hold back something this true. "I loved you a long time ago, and I still do."

"I love you, Sawyer. Always have. Always will."

There is no rush, only the quiet discovery of each other. The night stretches long, stitched together by whispers and laughter and the kind of closeness that feels like coming home.

And when sleep finally comes, I am wrapped in his arms, certain of only this: for the first time in a very long time, I look forward to another day.

# TWENTY-ONE

**Sawyer**

SUNLIGHT FILTERS THROUGH the blinds, painting soft stripes across the bed. For a moment I don't move, letting myself rest in the unfamiliar luxury of waking without dread pressing against my chest. Jake's arm is draped over me, heavy and protective, and Hattie lies curled at the foot of the bed like she's guarding us both.

I turn my head and find him watching me, his expression unguarded in a way that makes my heart twist.

"Good morning," he says, his voice rough with sleep.

"Morning." My voice is softer than I intend, like I'm afraid to break the spell.

He reaches over and brushes his fingers through my hair. "You okay?"

I nod. "Better than okay."

Something in his face eases, like he's been waiting a long

time to hear that. He leans over, kisses me slow, unhurried, as if we have all the time in the world.

We linger there, wrapped in the kind of silence that doesn't need filling. The lake outside is impossibly still, a mirror catching the early light.

"Coffee?" he finally asks.

"Only if you're making it," I tease.

He laughs, kisses my forehead, and disappears into the kitchen. I lie there, listening to the quiet sounds of a morning I didn't think I'd ever want to see. The kettle's whistle, Hattie's nails clicking across the hardwood, the low hum of a song playing from Jake's phone.

When he returns, he sets a mug on my nightstand and slides back in beside me. We sip, shoulders brushing. The coffee is warm, steadying. And for the first time in what feels like forever, I let myself imagine tomorrow.

The quiet stretches, comfortable but edged with something tentative. Finally, Jake says, "Last night..." He stops, then shakes his head. "I don't even know what to call it."

"Perfect," I offer, though my chest tightens with the weight of what comes next.

He looks at me, steady, serious. "I don't want to mess this up, Sawyer. I don't want to move too fast and scare you off."

I set my cup down, curl my knees up under me. "You're not the only one who's scared. I don't even know what I'm capable of... what I can promise."

His hand finds mine, thumb moving slow across my skin. "I'm not asking for promises. Just... let's see where it goes. One step at a time."

The simplicity of it, the patience in his voice, steadies something in me I didn't realize was shaking.

"Okay," I whisper.

He leans over, presses his lips to my temple. We sit like that for a long time, two people treading carefully over the fragile bridge between what was and what might be.

## TWENTY-TWO

**Jake**

AFTER SAWYER LEAVES, the house feels strangely quiet. Hattie pads after her, watching through the screen door until her Jeep disappears up the drive. Then she trots back to me, tail wagging, as if to say she knows something important has shifted.

I stand there a moment, taking it in, the morning light on the lake, the faint scent of coffee still in the air. It's ridiculous, maybe, how different everything feels this morning. Like the ground has tilted and, somehow, steadied at the same time.

I catch myself smiling. Smiling in a way I haven't in longer than I care to admit.

How unpredictable life is. I'd stopped believing it could surprise me with anything good. And then Sawyer shows up again, out of nowhere, like the missing piece I didn't know I was still waiting for.

It's hard to believe she's in my life again, after all the years we lost. Harder still to believe that last night happened, that she chose to stay. That she slept in my arms through the night.

I want to hold on to that, to believe in it, in her, in us.

But a voice at the back of my mind whispers caution. The world doesn't make promises. And I've seen how fast it can all be taken away.

Still, I can't shake the thought that maybe this, Sawyer, me, the way we fit together again, isn't an accident. Maybe it's a second chance I never expected to get.

Is it wrong to want to let go of the fear? To stop questioning and just believe in what we've found?

I want to. I really want to.

I grab my keys, whistle for Hattie, and head out to the truck. The morning air smells of damp earth and cut grass. We made a date for the hardware store, a normal kind of Saturday I never imagined having with her.

Ten minutes later, I turn down Sawyer's road. She's waiting on the porch, sunlight catching her hair, and I'm happy. Just happy.

# TWENTY-THREE

**Sawyer**

WE DRIVE TO West Lake in Jake's truck, Hattie sitting up on the seat between us, taking in our surroundings with the kind of joyous expression that makes Labs such wonderful companions.

I reach over to rub under her chin. She gives me an affectionate lick on the back of my hand. "She enjoys every moment of the day, doesn't she?"

"She does," Jake agrees. "That's how she sees life. It's an adventure one day to the next, and she can't wait to see the next thing we do together. It doesn't matter whether the sun is shining, or it's an overcast rainy day, she still sees plenty to enjoy."

"Dogs could give humans a lesson on that, couldn't they?"

"We could all learn a lot from Hattie."

We drive to the hardware store between West Lake and

Hales Ford Bridge. It takes us forty minutes or so to get there, and we ride with the windows down, country music playing on the AM radio. Jake parks near the front of the store, and we go inside, Hattie trotting between us on a leash. The employees there know her. A woman from the customer service desk walks up and gives her a treat, for which Hattie thanks her with an appreciative tail wag, chewing happily as we head for the lumber department.

Jake talks with the young man working there, telling him the number of boards and sizes we'll need to repair the dock. Once I've paid for the stack, we pull around back to the loading door, where two employees neatly arrange the boards in the back of Jake's truck.

"You may regret signing on for this," I say, glancing at the substantial pile of wood behind us as we pull away from the hardware store. "It will take a while to replace all of those."

"That's okay," Jake says. "I don't mind. We can do a little every day until it's done."

"I appreciate everything you've done to help me out. It's above and beyond the call of duty. I don't know how I'll pay you back."

"No payback needed," he says.

We head up 122, turn left a couple of miles out and end up on 834, the road that will take us back to Route 40. The road is two lanes and not very wide given the amount of traffic these days.

A rectangular white box truck pulls out from a side road just ahead. Jake hits the brakes, and the boards in the back slam forward. Hattie glances at Jake with a worried expression just as she's thrown from her seat onto the floorboard. I reach down and help her up.

"Sorry, girl," he says, rubbing her head. "We almost hit that guy. Are you okay?"

"Yeah," I say. "I'm fine. Did he not see us?"

"I don't know," Jake says, shaking his head and hanging back from the truck which is now weaving back and forth against the solid yellow line on the road.

"Do you think the driver is drunk?"

"Early in the day but could be."

We watch in silence for another minute from a safe distance. The truck drives straight for fifteen or twenty seconds and then begins to veer again, jerking back into his lane.

"Should we call 911?" I say, glancing at Jake.

"Yeah," he says, "This looks like something that might end badly."

Just then another car comes around the corner, and the truck veers into the driver's lane. The car hits its horn, shrieking past the truck, barely missing it.

I tap 911 on my phone, telling the operator who answers what we've just witnessed, hardly able to keep the urgency from my voice.

"Can you tell me your exact location, ma'am?"

Jake gives me the road names, and I relay them as calmly as I can.

"I'll alert any deputies in the area," she says.

"Thank you so much," I say and end the call.

"I don't want to get too close to him, but maybe I should try to go around and head him off?"

"That seems dangerous," I say.

"Yeah," he agrees. He starts to blow the horn then, pulling up closer behind the truck to get the driver's attention.

Just then, there's another bend in the road ahead. We're far enough back that I can see the car coming, a small white sedan.

My stomach drops as I feel what is about to happen even as we are unable to stop it.

"Jake! Watch out!"

The truck veers sharply into the other driver's lane. The car attempts to avoid it, but it's too late, and the truck hits it head on.

There's a loud boom announcing the impact of the truck with the car. Jake slams on the brakes, and we slide to a screeching halt.

This time, I have my arms wrapped around Hattie, holding her tight against me so that she doesn't fly into the dashboard.

Jake pulls the truck over, and we both jump out, leaving Hattie inside. I dread what we're about to see. I hang back a bit, fear washing over me in a tidal wave. Jake disappears around the back of the box truck, and I stand for a moment until the feeling of cowardice shames me into motion. I force myself to walk and then run. But what I see brings me to a halt. I gasp. The entire front left side of the sedan is under the enormous truck.

I instantly know the driver could not have survived this

impact. I stand staring at the wreckage, frozen in both body and mind. Jake is at the back door of the car, peering inside.

His voice is ragged when he says, "There's a little girl in the backseat."

I make my feet move, but they won't respond to the command from my brain.

"Sawyer," Jake calls out again. This time, I literally hurl myself forward, running now to the back of the car and willing myself not to think about anything beyond what I can do to help. "Is she—"

"It looks like she's unconscious," Jake says. "Here, let's get the door open. It's locked."

Jake looks around for something to break the back window. He grabs a rock from the nearby ditch. The child is on the other side of the back seat, and he taps the glass with the rock, then gives it a forcible crack. It breaks, and he reaches in to unlock the door, but it doesn't open. Jake lifts and pulls on the latch until it gives.

The girl, five years old or so, in a booster seat, is still strapped into her seatbelt. Her head droops to one side, and blood trickles from her nose. I force myself to look at the front of the car, where the impact was so great, crushing the front of the vehicle into the driver's space. There's a woman in the seat, but she's clearly not alive. Jake meets my stricken gaze, and I fight back a wave of nausea.

"Should we try to get the child out?" he asks, looking at me with an edge to his voice. "The car could catch on fire or—"

I struggle to think clearly. "Can you lift her out but keep her inside the car seat?"

"I'll try," he says. He slides across the backseat, unsnapping her seatbelt.

He tries to lift the car seat, but the top left edge is stuck under a piece of the car's door molding.

Jake tugs and pulls until he is finally able to free the seat, lifting the child up onto his lap, and then sliding back from the car. He stands, still holding her inside the seat and tight against him, looking at me. "What should we do?"

"Let's get her over on that bank of grass, off the road."

Just then a small red pickup truck pulls up. A man in a Franklin County Eagles baseball cap and overalls jumps out and runs toward us.

"Oh, my gosh," he says, looking horrified. "Is that Ava's car?"

"I don't know who it is," I say. "We were behind the truck when it had a head-on with this vehicle."

He glances at the child in Jake's arms, and tears begin to slide down his face. "That's Ava Miller. This is her granddaughter, Hannah. She takes her to preschool every morning. Where's Ava?"

"I'm sorry," I say. "The car was crushed—" I can't finish the sentence, and I know he doesn't need me to. His gaze now hangs on the vehicle wedged under the front of the box truck, and a look of profound sadness descends over him. I feel the depth of it, and I'm flung back to the hospital in New York and the patient faces imprinted on my memory.

Sadness engulfs me just as Jake says, "Sawyer, we have to help her. Come on."

He sets the seat in the grass. I drop down onto my knees, pressing my fingers against her wrist pulse. I feel nothing.

"She's not breathing," I say. And then I let my instincts take over from there, thinking what I would do if I were in the ER, if this child were brought to me there. I feel for a pulse. There isn't one.

"Can you get her out of the seat, Jake?"

He struggles with the snap on the belt holding her in the seat. As soon as it loosens, he gently lifts her and places her on the grass. I begin to work as hard as I know how, as hard as I ever have, something frantic inside me screaming, "You can't lose her. You can't lose her."

And I won't. I work without conscious thought, determined to breathe life back into this child. I hear Jake say he's going to check on the driver of the truck. I keep working until the child coughs and gasps for air. Her eyes flutter open. And she looks at me, her voice quivering when she says, "Grandma. Where's my grandma?"

My heart drops, and I feel the blood leave my face. The horror of what has happened here is beyond anything I can imagine a child this age having to process. I block her view of the wreckage with my body. "You're okay, Hannah. I'm a doctor, and you've been in a car accident, but the ambulance will be here soon, and they'll get you to the hospital to be checked out."

Her lips part, a question in her eyes. But before she can form the words, they flutter closed again. Jake is back. I look up, remembering the truck's driver. Jake shakes his head, somber. Grief again descends over me, and I pray the paramedics will be here soon. Maybe it's better that the child isn't aware of her surroundings at this point. What has happened is too terrible for words.

Jake puts a hand on my shoulder, squeezes hard. "Are you all right?"

"Yeah," I say.

"You saved her life."

I glance at the car behind us, my stomach lurching again at what has happened to this child's grandmother.

We meet eyes, and I see that he is feeling everything I'm feeling. There aren't any words to put to it to make it more real than it is. He takes my hand, links his fingers through mine, pressing hard, as if he knows I need this connection. "I know," he says. "I know."

# TWENTY-FOUR

**Sawyer**

THE AMBULANCE ARRIVES within minutes, its siren blaring long before it comes into view.

Two paramedics leap from the front, a third from the back. One runs toward us, gear in hand. "What have you got?" he calls, scanning the wreckage. "Anyone alive in there?"

I shake my head. "The driver's gone. The child, her granddaughter, I think, was unconscious. I gave her CPR. She's breathing now. I'm an ER doctor. Was," I amend softly.

The EMT nods quickly and kneels beside the girl. He checks her pulse, then her pupils. Two others follow with a stretcher, working swiftly to stabilize her neck and lift her carefully into the back of the ambulance. Their calm professionalism steadies me.

They thank us quietly before driving away, and then a

young county deputy approaches. He can't be more than twenty-eight. His eyes keep drifting to the crushed car.

"The coroner's on the way," he says. "And the wrecker too."

"We were behind the truck," Jake says. "Saw it weaving all over the road. There was one close call, a car coming around a curve barely missed it. That's when Sawyer called 911."

I nod, still feeling the weight of the phone in my hand. "The truck crossed the line. It hit the woman's car head-on."

The deputy shakes his head. "If she'd been speeding, the girl probably wouldn't have made it." He glances at the cab. "I didn't smell alcohol. But these guys drive all night sometimes. He could have nodded off."

Jake nods, somber. "Could have."

The deputy scribbles on his clipboard. "Can I get your names and numbers in case we need to follow up?"

We give him our information. Then we climb back in Jake's truck. The tires crunch over gravel as we pull away, the siren fading behind us. Hattie licks our faces, whining softly, as if she knows the terrible thing that has happened. I put a hand on her head and rub softly. Jake reaches out and strokes her side. Our hands meet, and I slip my palm over his, the three of us absorbing comfort from each other. We ride like that the rest of the way home.

## TWENTY-FIVE

**Jake**

SAWYER AND I make a half-hearted attempt at the dock repairs, but the morning has already emptied us. We stack the boards and leave the rest for another time.

I head back to my house, not because I don't want to be with her, but because the grief has become too much to carry in company.

Alone, it hits me now.

The randomness. The finality. The sheer cruelty of it. One moment, a woman is driving her granddaughter to preschool. The next, she's gone. No warning. No chance to say goodbye.

And that child, waking to a world without the person she trusted most.

I sit on the edge of the bed and drop my head into my

hands. And let the tears come. For the loss we witnessed. For the helplessness. And for Sawyer, because now, I understand.

I understand the exhaustion that must come from carrying that kind of loss day after day. The quiet way it breaks you down. No wonder she left the hospital. No wonder she felt like she couldn't keep going.

I don't regret what I've said to her—about hope, about healing. But I understand now. I reach for my phone and dial before I can talk myself out of it. She answers on the second ring.

"Hey," I say.

"Hey."

There's a pause. The kind that feels like it's holding something fragile.

"There's something I need to say," I tell her.

"What is it?"

"This morning—seeing what we saw—it made me realize I assumed too much. I thought I understood what you've been through. What it must have felt like to keep watching people die. I didn't. And I'm sorry if I ever came across like I had any idea what that cost you."

Her voice comes gently through the line. "You didn't. Jake, you have nothing to apologize for."

I don't speak. I let her keep going.

"I'm just glad it was you," she says softly. "If I had to go through something like that, I can't think of anyone else I'd rather have been with."

Her words settle over me. For the first time in hours,

something inside me eases a little. And the bond between us deepens.

# TWENTY-SIX

**Sawyer**

THE FOLLOWING MORNING, I drive over to Carl's to fill up my car and grab a few groceries. I'm low on staples and decide I'd rather avoid the bigger grocery store in town.

At the pump, I insert my credit card and wait while the tank fills. The air is cool and still, and for a moment, I wonder what Jake is doing today. He didn't mention coming over. I tell myself not to expect anything, but the thought still lingers.

I glance at the mask on my passenger seat and decide not to wear it. Inside the store, I'm not the only customer forgoing the mask. I think we're all tired of what it represents: fear and its reluctance to let go of us.

I grab what I need, milk, eggs, a loaf of bread, bananas, and another jar of peanut butter, then head to the register.

The same woman is behind the register. She smiles when

she sees me. It's nice to see her smile and know that she sees mine.

"How are you today?" she asks, ringing up my items.

"I'm good," I say. "You?"

"Can't complain," she says, then studies me more closely. "Oh. Wait. Are you the doctor who helped with that accident on 834 yesterday?"

"Yes," I say, surprised. "I am."

She places a hand over her heart. "God bless you, dear. I can't even imagine."

"Yeah," I say quietly. "It was tragic."

She nods. "Such a shame. You get in the car, thinking you'll be back home in ten minutes, and..." She trails off. We both understand.

"And that little girl..." she continues. "The way people are talking, I reckon she'll end up in the foster care system."

I blink. "What?"

The woman sighs. "Her grandma, the driver, was her only relative around here. That poor child's mother died when the girl was just a baby. Overdose," she adds, lowering her voice.

"Oh," I say, fresh sorrow washing over me. "Surely there's someone..."

"I hear the grandmother has a sister who moved to Georgia a long time ago. Apparently, she's in a nursing home though and wouldn't be able to care for her."

"That's awful."

"It is," she says. "I just hope she ends up somewhere kind." She finishes bagging my items and hands them over. "Thank you again for what you did."

I murmur my thanks and leave the store.

In the car, I sit for a moment, absorbing the weight of what I've just learned. I pull out of the parking lot and start driving.

I don't think about where I'm headed until I turn into Jake's driveway.

I park beneath the shade of an old tree. Across the field, I spot him near the strawberries. Hattie sees me first and runs, tail wagging, to meet me.

"Hey, girl," I say, bending to rub her head. She sits at my side like she's been waiting for me all morning.

Jake waves from the field and walks toward us. We meet halfway.

"Hey," he says, a little breathless.

"Hey."

"Everything okay?"

"I went to Carl's to get gas and a few groceries, and..."

His eyes search mine. "What is it?"

"The woman at the register told me something I didn't know. That little girl... she doesn't have any living relatives. Her grandmother was all she had."

Jake's face changes, his mouth tightening, eyes dimming. He looks like I felt when I first heard it.

"That's terrible," he says.

"It's unimaginable."

He's quiet for a moment, and then, "I guess they'll place her in foster care?"

"I assume," I say, though the words feel heavy and insufficient.

Silence settles between us, thick and weighted by yesterday's tragedy. Then Jake speaks again.

"A guy from the volunteer rescue squad called me last night," he says. "He said they think she's going to be okay. But she's still in the hospital."

A quiet pause passes between us before I ask, "Do you think we could go see her?"

He looks surprised by the question, then nods. "I don't know if they'll let us in, but we can bring something for her. Want to go now?"

"Yes," I say. "I really do."

"And the day came when the risk to remain tight in a bud was more painful than the risk it took to blossom."
— **Anaïs Nin, Diaries, Vol. 1**

# TWENTY-SEVEN

**Sawyer**

WE STOP AT a gift shop in town to pick up a few things for Hannah, a soft, plush basset hound with droopy ears and big, soulful eyes, and a pair of pink footie pajamas. I guess at her size, hoping they'll fit.

The hospital is smaller than the ones I worked in, but something about it feels steady. Solid. Like it belongs here in this community.

Before walking in, Jake and I put on masks, a sign at the front door declaring them mandatory. At the front desk, a volunteer, a woman with soft white hair and kind blue eyes, smiles from behind the glass.

"Can I help you?" she asks.

Jake speaks first. "We were hoping to visit the little girl who was in the car accident yesterday."

The woman nods, her expression sobering. "Hannah

Thompson. Visitors are restricted to immediate family. But... apparently, she doesn't have any listed."

Just then, a man in a white coat walks past the desk, eyes on a clipboard. He glances up.

"Oh, hey, Jake."

"Hey, Robert." Jake gestures toward me. "This is my friend, Dr. Sawyer Blakely. Sawyer, this is Dr. Murphy."

"Nice to meet you," we say at the same time, nodding instead of shaking hands.

"You're here about the child, I assume?"

"Yes," Jake says. "We brought a few things and wanted to check on her. But it sounds like we can't see her?"

Dr. Murphy glances at the volunteer. "Given the circumstances, come with me. Let's see what we can do."

We follow him down a long hall to the elevator, and then through a set of doors he opens with a key card. As we ride, he makes quiet small talk, asking about my work in New York. Whether I plan to return.

"I don't think so," I say, the answer coming more easily than I expected.

"I imagine it was tough," he says.

"Yes," I reply, and leave it at that.

As if he can sense the weight behind my silence, Jake presses a warm hand to the center of my back. Just once. Just enough. Tears threaten, but I blink them back.

We exit onto a quiet hallway. Dr. Murphy leads us to a room on the left, knocks gently, and opens the door. He gestures for us to step inside.

The girl in the bed looks impossibly small. Her face

pale. A bruise under one eye. Her chest rises and falls slowly beneath the blanket. Dr. Murphy steps to her side.

"Good morning, Hannah," he says. "How are you feeling?"

She studies him for a moment before answering in a soft voice, "Okay."

"These are the two people who helped you yesterday after the accident," he says. "They brought you a few things and wanted to check in on you."

Her eyes find mine first, then Jake's. They're solemn. Older than they should be.

"Hi, Hannah," I say.

Jake hands me the plush basset hound, and I place it gently on the bed beside her. "We thought you might like someone to keep you company."

I immediately regret the wording. But her eyes light up, just a little, and she runs a hand across the dog's soft head.

"Thank you."

She looks up at me again. "I remember you. After the wreck. You helped me breathe."

"Yes," I say, my throat tight. "That's right."

"Did you see my grandma?"

The question slices through me. I freeze. Jake steps forward, his hand on my back.

"Hi, Hannah," he says, emotion roughening his voice. "We did."

"Did you try to help her?"

"We wanted to. Very much."

"I saw the truck," she says. "Grandma tried to get out of the way, but it was too late. It hit us."

"I know," I say. "We were right behind you. There was nothing she could have done. But I'm certain her quick thinking saved your life."

She's quiet for a moment, processing. Then tears begin to slide down her cheeks.

"I don't want to be here without her."

Her shoulders tremble, her lip quivers. The sobs come quietly, shaking her small frame. I ache to climb into the bed beside her, to wrap her in my arms.

"Sometimes," I say, kneeling beside the bed, "the people we love have to go on before us. And it's the hardest thing in the world. I understand. I lost my brother when I was young."

She watches me with wide, solemn eyes, as though she's trying to understand something she doesn't yet have the words for.

"So where will I go?" she whispers, her eyes wide. "I don't have anyone else."

The question breaks me open. I don't know the answer.

"You're not alone, Hannah," I say. "I promise. We won't let you be alone."

There's a long pause. She studies me, really studies me, as if weighing whether she can believe those words. Then her fingers curl slowly around mine.

"Did your brother have blonde hair like you?" she asks, her voice small.

I blink, caught off guard, but moved.

"He did," I say softly. "And kind eyes. Like yours."

Something in her eyes shifts as she curls her fingers around mine.

She's reaching out from inside her sorrow.

The tiniest evidence. But enough.

And I know this: I will not let her disappear into a system that doesn't know her name, her laugh, or her grief. I won't. I can't.

## TWENTY-EIGHT

**Jake**

WE'RE BOTH QUIET for the first stretch of the drive back to the lake, the silence filled with the weight of the morning.

Sawyer speaks first. "Do you think I'm crazy for making that promise to her?"

"No," I say. "I understand how you feel. It tears me up to think about what she's facing."

"I can't imagine her walking out of that hospital into a home full of strangers. But I don't know how to stop that from happening."

She goes quiet again, staring out the window. Then, almost to herself: "I wonder what it takes to become a foster parent?"

The question catches me off guard.

"I'm not sure," I say carefully. "Are you thinking about—?"

"I don't know what I'm thinking," she says quickly. "I probably sound like a complete basket case. One minute, I'm ready to walk away from everything. The next, talking about taking in a child."

"You don't sound like a basket case."

She gives me a skeptical look.

"I'm serious," I say. "You're a compassionate person, Sawyer. You helped save that little girl's life."

She watches me, quiet again. I can see her weighing my words, trying to decide whether to believe me or herself.

"I know there are good foster families out there," she says.

"There are," I agree. "But that doesn't mean you couldn't be one of them."

She shakes her head, turning back to the window. "It's a crazy idea. I'm not in any place to be making decisions for someone else's life."

"You could be."

She glances at me, surprised. "Jake—"

"Do you believe," I ask gently, "that God puts people in certain places at the exact moment they're meant to be there?"

She takes a breath. "Yes. I don't think it's a coincidence that we were the ones who came upon that accident. Maybe we were meant to help."

"Then maybe there's more to it than just that moment. Maybe there's something you're meant to consider."

She doesn't answer for a long beat. Then quietly, "I don't know how I could. I don't even know who I am right now."

"Then maybe this is how you start to find out."

She looks at me again, her expression uncertain but not closed.

"All I'm saying," I add, "is there's nothing wrong with looking into it. You're not committing to anything. But if you do, if it's something you want to explore, just know I'll support you. In whatever way I can."

And I mean it. I've never meant anything more in my life.

# TWENTY-NINE

**Sawyer**

AFTER WE GET back from the hospital, I pace the house like it's haunted. Maybe it is. Or maybe it's just me, still full of ghosts I haven't buried properly.

Michael. Tommy. My parents.

All the lives I couldn't save.

And now... Hannah.

She's not mine. Not by blood. Not by obligation. But that girl has imprinted herself into some tender, broken place inside me, and I can't seem to close the door around it. I told Hannah she wouldn't be alone. I meant it then. I still do. I just don't yet know what that means.

I sit on the edge of the bed, pull up Michael's note on my phone. His words still echo in my chest: "I don't know what our future looks like. But I know you're the only one I want in it."

He believed in me.

He trusted me with his heart, his hope.

And I couldn't save him.

I press the heels of my hands to my eyes, trying to block out the wave of doubt building behind my ribs.

What if I fail her like I failed him?

What if I promise Hannah safety, promise her a home, and I can't follow through? What if I lose her too?

I don't know how to mother a grieving child when I'm still grieving myself. My love feels rusted, unreliable. Like a door that doesn't close all the way in the rain.

She deserves more than that.

She deserves someone whole.

But whole is not a word I can claim. Not yet.

Maybe not ever.

Still, when I looked into her eyes at the hospital... I saw something I haven't seen in a long time.

Trust.

Tiny. Fragile. But real.

And I can't forget the way her hand curled around mine. As if I was something steady in her storm.

I've wanted to feel needed again. I just didn't expect that need to come wrapped in a pink hospital gown and eyes too old for her age.

---

THE DREAM WAKES ME.

I lie still, staring into the darkness, heart pounding like

I'm in the middle of that climb up Smith Mountain. Sweat slicks my skin. It takes a moment to remember where I am.

I'm not in New York.

I'm here.

At the lake.

I blink up at the ceiling, sunlight still hours away. I glance at the clock—4:02 a.m.

There's no going back to sleep.

I get up, pad to the bathroom, splash cool water on my face. Then I make my way downstairs to the kitchen and start a pot of coffee.

When it's done, I pour a cup and carry it out onto the deck. The sky is still deep blue-black, the lake barely visible in the low light. It lies quiet and undisturbed, like a held breath.

A light mist floats across the surface, thin and curling, lifting slowly as the sky hints at dawn.

It's peaceful out here, softer than the silence I knew in New York. That silence felt like abandonment. This one feels like invitation.

I take a sip of coffee, the warmth grounding me, and I breathe deeply.

The fog is clearing.

On the lake.

And maybe, inside me too.

Can I really change Hannah's life?

And mine?

Am I capable now of doing something that bold, something that hopeful?

I try to picture it.

Her here. With me.

Waking up in the guest room. Sitting at this table. Laughing. Asking questions.

The old me could have done it. The one who believed she could fix what was broken if she worked hard enough. But I'm not sure that woman still exists.

Or maybe...maybe she does.

Maybe she's been buried.

Waiting.

Not that long ago, I didn't want to see another day. I'd lost so much, my patients, my career, the man I loved. A pandemic out of nowhere stripped away all the scaffolding I'd built my life on. But somehow, here I am.

And now there is this unexpected widening in my chest. A soft shift. A slow opening.

A child who needs someone.

A man who once knew me better than anyone.

A life I never imagined, suddenly within reach.

It doesn't look like the future I planned.

But maybe, just maybe, I'm becoming someone who can step into it anyway. Scarred, unsure. But standing. Still standing.

# THIRTY

**Jake**

I HEAR A vehicle pull into the driveway and glance out the window.

Hattie trots to the door, tail wagging. I follow her outside, and we meet Sawyer just as she's getting out of her car.

She smiles, and there's something lighter about her this morning. Something different.

"Hey," I say.

"Hey." She bends to rub Hattie's head. "I should've called."

"You know you don't have to." I gesture toward the house. "Want a cup of coffee?"

"I've had enough for today. I've been up since four." She pauses. "Can we talk?"

"Of course." I nod toward the back field. "Walk with me to check the berries?"

We cross the yard, unhurried. The air is warm and soft, the kind of morning that feels like a new beginning.

"It's beautiful," she says.

"Perfect," I agree.

We reach the field, and I pluck a ripe berry, hand it to her. "First one of the season."

"They'll all be ready soon?"

"Within a few days. I'll be out here every morning."

"I'd love to help," she says.

"I'd love that too."

She's quiet. I let the silence stretch, knowing she'll speak when she's ready.

"I had the dream again," she says finally. "The one where I leave here and go back to New York. I woke up shaking."

I take her hand. Squeeze once.

"There's something I need to confess," she says. "When I came here... I wasn't planning to stay. I came to say goodbye. To everything. To life, I think. I didn't want to keep going. I thought the world was too broken. That I was too broken."

I absorb this admission, realizing I am not shocked by it. "I suspected," I say.

She looks at me, her eyes full with tears. "You helped me remember what life can be. You helped me believe in good things again."

"You're one of the strongest people I've ever known, Sawyer. What you've seen, it would have broken anyone. But you didn't stay broken."

She looks up, meets my gaze.

"Can I tell you one of my truths?" I ask.

She nods.

"I lost everything, too. My career. My sense of who I was. But if all of that led me back to you, then I wouldn't change a thing."

Fresh tears pool in her eyes.

"I never thought life would feel this way again. But somehow, it seems... possible."

I reach out and brush a tear from her cheek.

"I love you, Sawyer. However this looks, whatever pace it takes, we'll walk it together."

She places her hands on my chest. "I love you." She kisses me. Soft, then deeper.

And everything shifts.

In the middle of the ripening strawberry field, Hattie barks once, tail wagging fast and hard.

Sawyer laughs and reaches down to rub her head. "We'll share him, okay?"

We stand there, arms wrapped around each other, surrounded by the slow, steady promise of the harvest ahead.

The morning is bright.

And everything, pretty much everything, even in this scarred world we call home, feels possible.

"In the depth of winter, I finally learned that within me there lay an invincible summer."
— **Albert Camus, "Return to Tipasa"**

# EPILOGUE
## TWO YEARS LATER

**Sawyer**

IT'S THE KIND of late summer day that reminds me why I love this place.

The sun is high, the sky endlessly blue, and cicadas hum in the trees. We're back in Bull Run Cove, where the water is glass smooth. Ideal conditions for Hannah's water-skiing lesson.

She's been working on it for weeks, determined. Jake is patient with her, his voice never losing its calm.

"There you go," he calls, tossing her the rope. "Keep the edge of your ski angled once you're up."

"Okay, Daddy. I think I've got it."

She started calling us "Mama" and "Daddy" a while ago. The words just came one day, unannounced but completely right. Her choice, her timing.

Jake and I got married over a year ago, nearly a year

after I finalized Hannah's adoption. Because I'd been the doctor who helped her at the scene of the accident, and because the county's social worker knew my family's long roots here, the foster approval process moved faster than I ever imagined possible. After the wedding, Jake adopted her too.

The process wasn't without its struggles. Nothing about the last two years has been. There were home visits and pressing, painful interviews, nights when Hannah couldn't sleep from nightmares, mornings when I questioned whether I was strong enough for any of it. But I know that healing doesn't follow a straight line. And little by little, we found our way forward.

There are moments, like this one today, where I still can't quite believe where I am. Who I am. What we've become.

Jake sits beside me in the boat, steady, kind, quietly strong. I look at our daughter, cutting across the lake. I think about Hattie, tail wagging from her perch at the back of the boat.

And I feel... peace.

It's not that I think nothing bad will ever happen again. Of course, I know better than that. We're all temporary here, and pain is a recurrent visitor.

But I believe in now. In this moment. In the life the four of us have together.

I volunteer two days a week at a local free healthcare clinic. The work grounds me.

At the clinic, I still see the aftershocks, lungs that never fully healed, families still unraveling, grief that shows up in quiet, unspoken ways. But I also see resilience. And that helps.

I let myself remember on a regular basis. Not to reopen wounds, but to honor the people I couldn't save. To remind myself why I keep showing up.

And sometimes, before the house is awake, I walk the rows of the strawberry field.

It's peaceful in the early light. The dew clings to the leaves. The air smells like soil and sweetness.

There's something sacred about those rows. Something honest.

Jake says strawberries are stubborn. That they'll survive a frost when they shouldn't. That they come back even after a burn, growing through the ash, quietly beginning again.

Sometimes I think I understand them better than I understand myself.

There was a time, not so long ago, when I didn't believe anything would grow in me again. Not joy. Not purpose. Not love.

But here we are.

The strawberries came back.

And so did I. So did we.

Hannah wipes out mid-run, tumbling with a splash. From her seat at the back of the boat, Hattie barks frantically until Jake slows the boat and circles back. She watches, waiting, until we reach Hannah again.

"I'm okay, Hattie!" Hannah calls out, laughing as she swims.

That bond between them—it's something special. Hattie's

claimed Hannah's room as her own. No one asked her to. She just knew where she was needed most.

Sometimes, when Hannah skis, she uses Tommy's old water ski. She knows it was his. One afternoon while we sat at the dock, I told her what a great skier he was, his ski resting beside us like a time capsule.

"He was brave," she said, running her fingers over the worn bindings. "I want to be like that," she added, without looking up.

And I remember thinking—she already is.

Hannah still has hard days. She grieved her grandmother deeply. We visit her grave site regularly, and Hannah takes flowers. Over time, with help and space, she's come to believe it's okay to feel joy again. And sometimes, it's braided with sadness. That's okay, too.

"I think I'm done for now!" she shouts.

Jake reaches down to lift her onto the boat.

"That was awesome," he says.

She grins. "Not awesome yet, but I'm getting there."

"I think you're awesome," Jake says, squeezing her shoulder. He hands her a towel, then turns to me. "You skiing?"

"I think I'm in a floating mood today," I say. "Too peaceful not to just float."

"Floating it is," Jake says. He pulls out life jackets from under the seat, straps one on Hattie, and we all step onto the platform.

"Ready," Hannah says. "Set. Go!"

We dive in.

Hattie belly-flops into the water and swims straight for

Hannah, circling her once, then chasing water bugs across the surface.

"She never catches them," Hannah says. "But she really tries."

Jake chuckles. "I think they like teasing her."

We float side by side, sunlight dancing on the water. Jake slips an arm around my waist, and I rest my head lightly against his shoulder.

From a few feet away, Hannah treads water, watching minnows flash below her toes.

"Mama?" she says. "Can we do that picnic float again this weekend? The one where we tie up to the dock and just read books and eat snacks?"

I smile.

Two years ago, she would never have asked for something like that. Grief and guilt have a way of making us think we don't deserve joy.

"I'd love that," I say. "We'll make it a tradition."

Jake leans in and kisses my temple. "Perfect day," he says.

"It really is."

I kiss him, softly, slowly. When we pull apart, I whisper, "Thank you."

"For what?"

"For loving me. For believing this life was still possible."

He smiles. "Thank you," he says, brushing my cheek. "For trusting me. For believing in me."

We roll onto our backs and float, the sun warm on our faces, the lake wrapping around us like a promise.

It's not a perfect world.

Far from it.

There's sorrow. There's loss. Unimaginable pain at times.

But there's also love.

And for me, for us, that's reason enough.

To stay.

To hope.

To begin again. Renewed. Like Jake's strawberry field.

## AUTHOR'S NOTE

When I first began writing this story, I wasn't sure what it was going to be. I only knew I wanted to explore a quiet grief for the things we consider our failures, the kind that sits beneath the surface of a person's life, unspoken and unresolved. As the story unfolded, it became clear that The Strawberry Field wasn't just about loss. It was about resilience. About how we draw both sorrow and hope from the same vein. About what it means to come home, even when we don't think it exists anymore.

Sawyer's journey was born from a question I kept asking myself during the early days of the COVID-19 pandemic: How do we keep going when the world no longer feels safe? We all watched as medical professionals shouldered unimaginable burdens. We listened to stories of isolation, of helplessness, of deep and lasting fatigue. And I knew I wanted to honor that experience, not with headlines, but through the story of a character who was deeply human. Flawed, grieving, and unsure if she could still find her way.

During those same years, I also found myself unable to release a new book. Part of that was my own struggle, to come to terms with how I now see the world, and to reconcile the stories I tell with the realities we've lived through. Writing this novel was, in many ways, how I began to make peace with that.

The pandemic is not the centerpiece of this novel, but it is its shadow. It shaped Sawyer's loss of identity, her disillusionment with the world, and ultimately, her slow, tentative return to hope. It sits quietly in the background—where grief so often does.

This story is also about love. Romantic love, yes, but also the kind that finds its way into unexpected places, between a man and a dog, between a grieving heart and a healing child, between the version of ourselves we thought we had to be and the one we're learning to become.

To anyone who has walked through grief, burnout, or the slow rebuilding of a life, this story is for you. I hope it reminds you that there is always another chapter, another morning, another reason to keep showing up.

With gratitude and hope,

Inglath

## FOR ANYONE WHO NEEDS SUPPORT

If Sawyer's story resonated with you because of your own loss, burnout, or thoughts of giving up, please know this: help exists, and hope remains. You are not alone.

In the United States, you can call or text 988 to reach the Suicide and Crisis Lifeline, available 24 hours a day, or visit 988lifeline.org.

If you're outside the U.S., international helplines can be found at findahelpline.com.

Made in United States
Cleveland, OH
02 December 2025